Angels All Around

Alice Burnette Greene

Thank you
Maywood Public
Library!
Alice Greene

iUniverse, Inc.
New York Bloomington

Angels All Around

iUniverse books may be ordered through booksellers or by contacting:

iUniverse
1663 Liberty Drive
Bloomington, IN 47403
www.iuniverse.com
1-800-Authors (1-800-288-4677)

ISBN: 978-1-4502-5145-7 (pbk)
ISBN: 978-1-4502-5147-1 (cloth)
ISBN: 978-1-4502-5146-4 (ebk)

Library of Congress Control Number: 2010911825

Printed in the United States of America

iUniverse rev. date: 9/16/2010

Chapter 1

She is an Angel on her way to existence in the created world. It was about time for her to leave. "This time," her thoughts spoke to her partner, "I'll make it. I won't fail like last time." She refined that thought. "Well, I didn't actually fail. I just didn't do everything I meant to accomplish. I wish it wasn't so hard to remember." She will soon enter a human embryo through the process of translation, leaving the heavenly realm and entering into the time-bound created world called earth.

The breath of life of every human embryo comes from being inspirited by an angelic host. Without inspiriting, humans would have no sentient perception of the heavenly realm: no ability to think abstractly, reason, conjecture, theorize, create, acknowledge beauty, or recognize things theological. When the angelic hosts enter the created world, all knowledge of their heavenly existence is gone. Yet, the hosts are sent into the world with things to do, assigned to them by the Creator. They must remember who they are and what it is they are to do.

The Creator's Plan is for creation to be connected to but not controlled by the spiritual forces, which include the angelic hosts and their enemies, the Opposers. When the Angels in the world are successful in remembering what they are to do, they will ultimately bring the whole world back in sync with the Creator's Plan. The Opposers' goal is to keep the Angels distracted and to prevent them from returning to the Creator. This spiritual warfare takes place on the battleground of human souls.

This time she left with a new hope and joy. She was determined. She shared her thoughts with her partner, the one she is to join in the world with a shared purpose. "This time I'll be stronger. I won't be fooled or misled. Not this time." She gathered in herself the gifts assigned to her by the Creator, healing and great compassion, both greatly needed in the time and place she was entering. She sent encouraging farewells to her partner and began the translation. The entry was smooth; she found her place with relative ease. Then all awareness was gone. She was born on the south side of Chicago in 1972, earth time, née Kenisha Brown, only daughter of Essie Mae Brown, an eighteen-year-old single mother and foster child.

Kenisha

"Hey, angel! I could use a good massage right now." That was Marvin. Half of his right leg had been blown off by a roadside bomb when he was on patrol in Baghdad. The other leg was wounded with a deep gash that severed sinew and nerves. They had worked hard to keep that one working for him, and it was getting better. He was only twenty-three years old. Full of anger and self-pity, he was brought in a month ago to the rehab unit and assigned to Kenisha for physical therapy. She refused to buy into his self-pity, treating him with total irreverence. She told him that he needed to get over it, that it could have been a lot worse. But she also told him that he was a hero, that he was brave, and that those things said a lot about him. His bravery would stay with him for the rest of his life, to share with his children and his grandchildren. She told him that he would heal, that he had his whole life ahead of him, and that he'd be able to kick a football farther than anybody with a real leg.

Marvin, like the rest of the patients in rehab, responded well to Kenisha's touch and her voice. Something about her was soothing. There was strength in her hands when she manipulated the muscles that didn't want to work anymore, but in that strength there was also a gentleness that seemed to be a part of her personality. When she spoke, when she touched, even when she looked at them, they seemed to feel the healing taking place, both mentally and physically.

"I'll send Nurse George over to take care of you right away, Marvin. And stop calling me angel," she shot back.

"I don't want no man rubbing on me. Come on, angel, just ten minutes. I won't tell your husband," he said.

She relented and walked over to him. "You're the one who better watch out for my husband. He's bigger than you. Roll over, and I'll work your leg for a bit." She had to keep from cringing when she looked at the deep gash in his lower leg.

"I'm next," said Jorge. He was in the bed to the right of Marvin and had been in the unit for a month learning to walk again after having both his legs broken when his Humvee turned over on top of him after hitting a land mine.

"Me, too, angel," cried out Jonathan, the newest one, over in the left corner two beds away. He had come in paralyzed from the waist down, hit by a sniper.

Her heart went out to them. She wished she had more time to spend with them all, but there were fifty-three more like them just on this unit. "Jorge, tell your wife what you want. She'll be here today. And, Jonathan, it's your turn to go with me to work out, so don't give me any lip, or I'll give you a workout you won't ever forget."

"Aw, angel, you're so mean."

"Stop calling me angel!"

Kenisha had been working at the VA rehab unit for four years now. It was an old hospital, but this wing had been recently renovated. The renovations were intended to give the room a fresh, new look, but the bare, white walls, white-tiled floor, and harsh fluorescent lights, along with the beeping and binging of the medical robotics, made this room feel as antiseptic as it smelled. It was already filled beyond its intended capacity.

She navigated between the beds skillfully as she checked the charts and the patients with smooth and sure movements. There were too many guys in this room for her. When the hospital was first built, rooms like this one were intended for low-maintenance patients, those who were in the final stages of care before discharge. Kenisha knew that with the kind of injuries these soldiers were coming in with, they needed more privacy. *At least they have the curtains to separate their pain from each other*, she thought.

After kneading Marvin's leg for a minute, she went over to help Jonathan into the wheelchair beside his bed and told the other two to behave. She was just about to roll Jonathan out when two orderlies brought in the new patient for the fifth bed in the four-man room—a young guy who had just come from overseas.

After Jonathan's session, Kenisha rolled him back into the room and helped him into the bed. She stopped to look at the chart of the new guy, Michael Lindebloom, who was now in the bed between Jonathan and Marvin. They had removed one kidney and a part of his lower intestines to fix the hole in his side, he had a broken left arm, his left lower leg had been amputated, and he was bandaged from the lower part of his face down his neck to the upper part of his chest. Extensive skin grafts had been required to repair the burns. *He's lucky to be alive,* she thought as her heart went out to him. As she stood there, Michael began to stir from his deep sleep.

Chapter 2

He felt her absence. She had forgotten everything now. They named her Kenisha. He wished he would be able to remember that name. The Creator had given them their instructions. He and Kenisha were to meet, marry, and have a child. A "special" child. It seems so simple. But it's never easy. The world is so full of distractions. What is easy is to get misled and turned around, to lose focus. So many have failed. He and Kenisha can't afford to fail this time. He knew that the Opposers would do all they could to stop them. The Opposers are well-practiced and know all the weaknesses and shortcomings of the created beings.

He had to admit that failure is a real possibility. He reminded himself that if they do fail, the Creator's Plan would still be fulfilled—somehow. But he also knows that if they are able to remember and do their part, the Creator's Plan will move forward significantly. Otherwise, it could be Earth centuries before this part of the Plan is accomplished, and so many more of the children will be lost. They can't let the Opposers stop them this time.

Everything was set up for him now. He'll be born two years earlier and somewhere nearby where they'll be sure to meet. At least that's the plan. He knew the process well. With his will he found the right time, place, space, and person, and then he gathered his appointed gifts of righteousness, strength, and determination. Once the translation process started, he would no longer be in complete control. So everything had to be set up just right, and the timing had to be perfect. He turned his thoughts to the embryo that he was to enter and simply focused his being in that direction to start the translation process.

He never saw them coming. He was right, they were out in force. The Opposers waited just long enough for him to start the process, and then they moved a human host to drive a car while drunk, killing the planned human parent just as he was about to inspirit the fertilized egg in her womb. At that point in the inspiriting process, any other host would have gone back to the heavenly realm and worked out another plan. But that would have dramatically changed the plan, increasing the difficulty these two would have finding each other.

What the Opposers didn't know was that he had worked out an alternative plan, with the Creator's approval—not as good a human match for Kenisha as the original plan, but one that could be worked. With a mighty strength of determination and effort that had not been seen before, he turned away in mid-process and moved six earth-years ahead to the second human, who also didn't know that she was pregnant yet. He entered, and all awareness was gone. He was born Michael Lindebloom, the third son of Jewish parents Jeff and Sophie, in Brooklyn, New York, 1976.

The Opposers raged with anger. They were not finished with these two hosts.

Michael

The first thing he saw when he opened his eyes was her standing there above him, with the afternoon October sun shining in behind her through the dusty window. She had a short Afro haircut, dyed kind of platinum blondish, and through his haze, the sun shining from behind her made her hair look like a halo around her head. He vaguely wondered if he had died and gone to heaven. She turned, looked at him, and smiled. Something moved deep within him.

"Hey, soldier," she said gently. He couldn't open his mouth in response. She looked at his chart, then at him, and said, "You're gonna be just fine," and walked out. That deep place within him accepted her prognosis, and he fell back to sleep.

Around 4:00 PM Michael's consciousness was aroused again by the voice of the guy in the bed next to him. "Hey, angel, get me a beer, will you? I'm dying of thirst."

"Trust me, Marvin, I won't let you die. Here, have some apple juice," she said.

She really is an angel, Michael thought. His thoughts skittered around the idea of needing to be in a hospital in heaven, but it was too much. He tuned out again.

Michael woke about 7:00 PM with his parents and his brother, Charlie, standing around the bed staring emotionally at him. Dr. Brennan, the chief surgeon, had just reviewed Michael's situation with them. The truck carrying Michael's unit had been hit by a roadside bomb. Michael was sitting next to the driver, who was killed. Michael was thrown out of the front of the truck, the force of the bomb burning the flesh on the left side of his face and upper chest. His left arm was broken, and shrapnel cut through his torso injuring his intestines and kidneys as well as mangling his left leg. The only way to save his life was to remove the left leg below the knee and to remove his left kidney and some of his intestines.

Michael's first lucid thought when he saw his family there was to wonder why his mother was crying. The dark mascara streaks down her cheeks, her red, puffy eyes, and the tight, wavering lips stretched into an unsuccessful smile belied her cheerful "Hi, baby." She was leaning on Dad, who held her tight and made no effort to show anything but concern.

Michael turned to look at Charlie on the other side of the bed, who smiled bravely and said, "Welcome back." Michael tried to open his mouth to speak, but he couldn't. Slowly he began to remember. As his mind climbed into awareness, he began to see it all over again: the soldiers in the truck, the bomb, the explosion. His mind went off like a siren as pictures of chaos, destruction, and fear broke through his semiconsciousness, like bombs going off all over again; he escalated into complete panic. He tried to shout out loud with his mind since he couldn't get his mouth to open, but the only thing his distraught family could see was the panic in his eyes. Michael struggled to pull out of the restraints of tubes and bandages, when a man in white came in seemingly from nowhere and authoritatively put his hand on Michael's forehead, ordered Michael to calm down, and shooed his family out.

"Michael, calm down," he ordered. "You're back in the States. You're having a flashback. It's just a flashback. Calm down."

The strength of his voice made its way through Michael's mental chaos. "You're back in Chicago, in the Veteran's Hospital. I'm Dr. Brennan." Dr. Brennan looked into Michael's eyes until he saw Michael's panic begin to subside.

Michael calmed down as commanded. He couldn't stop the tears from welling up and rolling down as if they had minds of their own. Everything came back to him now. Michael tried to lift himself up with his arms, but couldn't. He reached down with his right arm to try to find his leg, and he moaned.

The doctor saw him reaching and said more softly, "You're going to miss your leg. It's not unusual for you to feel like it's there. Don't worry, with a prosthesis, you'll be fine. You'll be here for several weeks. You've had skin graft surgery to repair the burns on your face and neck. That's why your face is wrapped. We expect you to look almost good as new when we're finished. You're a lucky guy, Michael. You're going to be just fine."

Hadn't somebody else told him that, or was it just a dream?

Dr. Brennan left, and Michael's family moved back to his bedside. Michael suffered through their attempts to be brave for a couple of hours, until he finally feigned sleep after dinner so that they would leave. He needed to be alone with his thoughts. He woke up from his pretend sleep around 8:00 AM, without having thought a thing, and there she was again, at the foot of his bed, the angel. "Hey, sleeping beauty," she said. "How ya feeling?" Her eyes and her lips moved into a smile that said she was happy to see him. She seemed to him, somehow, vaguely familiar.

Michael thought she was a nurse. There was something about her that he couldn't quite put his finger on. She was more attractive than she was pretty. The short, blonde Afro accentuated her coffee-with-cream skin. Her eyes were large and slightly almond-shaped, dark brown, and too deep to easily look into. Her generous smile opened up a dimple on her left cheek. She was pretty. But what grabbed him wasn't so much her looks. There was an aura about her, something that he couldn't grasp. It was just too hard to think. He still couldn't get his mouth or his mind to respond to her.

She seemed to know what he was thinking when she said, "I'm not a nurse. I'm your rehabilitation therapist. You'll spend a lot of time with me when you get a little stronger. We'll get you out of here in no time."

At that moment he was glad that he couldn't respond, because he didn't know what to say.

Chapter 3

The Opposers' thoughts were dark and always angry. The anger roiled around and clashed brutally into itself. Each time they intervened to destroy the enemy's plan, somehow they could never completely stop it. Their successes were many, though, and they continued to try, as they had since almost the beginning of time, and as they always will. Their purpose was no less than to return creation back to chaos, back to the deep dark, as it was before the beginning of created time. In order to do that, they had to turn as many angelic souls away from the Creator as possible.

The one called Michael was not supposed to be born. None of the heavenly hosts had ever seen a translation like that before. After the amazing translation into the new womb, the Opposers put the thought in the mother's head to abort him. She tried, but somehow he was hidden away deep inside and the procedure didn't reach him. She didn't know that it didn't work until it was too late for her to try again. The one called Kenisha should not have been born either. The Opposers thought they had destroyed her mother's womb by a previous abortion, but again the life force proved to be too strong.

Darkness

"Mom, I'm feeling a little tired right now. Would you mind if I just rested?" Michael was tired, but more tired from trying to make light conversation than anything else. He had been in the rehab unit for a week. At 4:00 PM, the weak light of this cloudy day was already waning, and so was his energy. His parents had been there since noon talking with him as well as the other patients, doctors, and caregivers. Michael's head wraps had been removed the day before; his skin grafts were healing well. He was able to talk, but he didn't want to. His parents' ability to make friends with everyone around him just seemed to grate on his nerves.

"Sure, sweetie. We'll leave and give you some rest." His mom bent over to kiss him on the forehead. "It's so good to see how well you're recovering. I am so encouraged by what the doctor is telling us. You'll be back on your … back up and around in no time. Won't he, Jeffrey?"

His father's voice was a little too cheery. "Sure will. You just keep on doing what the doctors tell you. They're good doctors here … they know what you need to do. They tell me they're going to fit you for a new leg soon and get you walking again."

He was about to say more, but Sophie nudged him, and he stopped.

"Bye now, baby," she said with an intentionally bright grin. "We'll be back tomorrow. Charlie said to tell you he'd be by this weekend, and Jonathan, too." As they went out the door, Michael could hear his mom start on his dad. "You shouldn't bring up his leg …"

He couldn't believe he was in here, torn and broken like a piece of old driftwood. How stupid he felt! He wanted to serve his country, and instead he was laid up with only one working arm and half a leg gone. Who knows what he was going to look like and feel like after he heals. What a moron! He wondered what kind of career he could possibly have now. He imagined himself hobbling around a courtroom, looking pitiful instead of impressive.

Michael thought about how excited he had been when he told his family that he'd enlisted in the army, even though he knew they thought he was nuts. His mom blamed his dad for it all—she always did. He remembered her saying for the millionth time what a shame it was they'd moved to Chicago from New York so that his dad could take that promotion. She never wanted to come. His parents had migrated to the close-in suburb on the north side of Chicago, Lincolnwood, from New York City in the early eighties in order for his father to take a promotion to vice president of the shoe company he worked for.

Jeff Lindebloom was hesitant to move, mainly because he knew that Sophie, who grew up in Brooklyn, would not want to go. She liked to remind him it was his choice, but they all knew that if she had put up a fuss about it, they wouldn't have moved. She didn't resist, though, because she was attracted by the money that he would make and she was seduced by the idea of being married to the vice president for the Midwest region of Goldberg's Shoes. So they made the move with the three boys in tow: Charlie, the oldest at twelve; Jonathan, nine; and Michael, seven. While the boys were growing up, she always let them know they were socially above the midwesterners.

You'd think she would be over all of that by now, but Michael figured it had become a family habit, her complaining and the rest of them turning a deaf ear and accepting that she would always complain. Michael thought that if Dad's job had just done better, maybe she wouldn't have complained so much. But after the first twelve years or so, by the mid-nineties, the shoe business began to slow, and while Jeff could still make a respectable living, they knew they wouldn't be able to pay for any of the boy's graduate school. And Michael wanted to be a lawyer.

So he joined the ROTC while an undergraduate and was fortunate to have been selected for reserve status and allowed to go to Northwestern's law school before being activated right after graduation. Michael knew what he wanted to do. He'd start with government service as a prosecutor for a few years and then move into civil service, possibly politics. And he knew that at this time in the country's history—after September 11, 2001—he couldn't do anything better than military service. He graduated from law school in May 2002, was inducted in June, was in Iraq by September, and now, in spite of all his best laid plans, he was back in Chicago at the VA Hospital in late October 2002.

His mom found a way to make everything that happened her father's fault. So, yes, he knew that she'd blame his dad by somehow connecting the move to Lincolnwood and the drop in his dad's salary with his joining the army and, consequently, the loss of his leg. What a screwed-up mess. Michael stayed in a funk most of his waking time in the hospital, driven by his weakness, physical pain, and mental anguish.

A short while after his parents left, Kenisha walked in to take another patient down to rehab. The other men in the room all seemed to want her attention at once, but Michael just watched her. She fascinated him, and he didn't really know why. She had only spoken to him a couple of times, checked on his progress chart, and asked him how he was doing. She always seemed to be moving about, but she never seemed to hurry a lot. And she always seemed happy. In his depression, Michael wondered what she had to be so happy about while she flitted and flirted around with all the other men in the room. Her happiness only made him feel worse, at least until she turned and spoke to him and once in awhile smiled at him. Somehow that lifted the film of his funk just a little higher.

Chapter 4

Michael and Kenisha were dangerous to the Opposers, for they held the key to a major change that would greatly move the Creator's Plan forward. The child these two would bear would have the potential of bringing millions more of the creatures back to the Creator. The Opposers gnarled and roiled around in anger at that thought. The Opposers had tried many times to prevent these two from meeting, but each time their plans had been thwarted. The accident, the rape, the abortion, the war, the bomb—so far nothing had kept them apart. But they had some success with one close to Kenisha, her husband Joe, whom she had married before she met Michael. The Opposers would continue to work that angle, using the creature's own religious traditions as well as their racial prejudices to keep these two distracted.

Sunshine

"Time to try out that new leg, Michael." Kenisha smiled as she stood at the side of his bed. Michael had been in the hospital for over two weeks. The skin grafts were healing well, and so was everything else, according to all the doctors. Everything was healing well except his mind. He still slept fitfully and heard the bomb going off next to him most every night. He still regretted all the decisions he made that got him here. He couldn't talk to his family about his regrets, because he knew that conversation would just drag up old and unresolved issues that would leave everyone at each others' throats. So he took it out on himself. His sullenness kept him from making friends with any of the other patients, and they respected his clear desire to be left alone. Kenisha had given him exercises to do for his left arm while in the bed, but Michael only worked at them halfheartedly, and then only because he wanted her to leave him alone. The only thing he had really worked at up to this point was getting into the wheelchair that sat next to his bed so that he could make it to the bathroom without any assistance.

She was there to take Michael to rehab. They were alone in the room. Both Marvin and Jorge had recently been discharged. Jonathan was out in the courtyard, taking advantage of an unusually warm early November day. Michael's prosthesis had been fitted the day before, but he was not inclined to try it. "I don't think I'm ready for that yet," he said as he sat up in the bed, avoiding her eyes. "This thing doesn't feel right. I think they need to fit it again," he mumbled. He wished she would just leave him alone.

Kenisha wouldn't let him off the hook. "Come on, soldier." She put her hands on her hips and looked directly at him. "Don't you want to get out of here? You've got your whole life ahead of you. Besides, I hear that bionic men are kind of hot these days." She smiled brightly.

He was not about to let her phony cheerfulness get to him. He kept staring in front of him at nothing, with a determined nothingness on his face. When he didn't respond, her smile faded. After a minute, she sat on the edge of his bed by his feet, not speaking. She sat there for what seemed like twenty minutes, looking at her nails, the walls, out the window, not saying anything.

He finally looked at her, and something moved again in his heart, but that just irritated him more. He shared his irritation with her when he said, "Don't you have somebody else to take care of?"

Flashing another bright smile, she almost laughed when she looked at him. "Nobody more important than you. Besides, you've just given me forty free minutes, so if you don't mind, I'll just rest here for a while." Her voice had a musical lilt that was pleasant to his ears in spite of his irritation.

He couldn't stand her sitting next to him like that without saying anything, and it was pretty clear to him that she was not going to move any time soon. "So, how long have you been working here?" he asked gruffly. It wasn't that he really cared; he just needed to say something.

"I started here about four years ago, after working over at the county hospital for a couple of years when I graduated from UIC."

"What kind of degree did you get?"

"A bachelor's in physical therapy."

"Do you like it?"

"Yeah, I do. But what makes it good for me is that I get to work with soldiers like you."

"Yeah, right. You like to see us all mangled up like this." he sneered.

She stopped smiling and looked in his eyes. "I think you know better than that. What's good is watching how the mangled bodies begin to heal and how your lives are put back together again. What's good is that I get to watch men like you get through the destruction and get to know that there's still hope. And it's good because I know that you are more blessed than you know, because you're still here. And you especially, Michael, really do have a whole life ahead of you. You're still young. You still have two arms. You just need to work on getting one of them back in use again." She stood and picked up his prosthesis, her voice insistent. "You lost one leg, but you'll have two when you get this prosthesis working right. And most importantly you still have your brain, although you seem to have got it stuck in a bad place that you need to get out of. You can do anything you want to do, Michael. You just need to get out of your past." She put the plastic leg down with a clump and folded her arms across her chest.

"Hmmph" was all he could come up with in response. Internally he resisted everything she said. *She thinks she knows what she's talking about. She doesn't know what a big screwup I am,* he thought.

His lack of response didn't stop her. "There's nothing that can't be corrected, Michael, as long as you're willing to deal with it." She paused for a moment, as if analyzing him, and said quietly while her eyes spoke sincerity, "There's nothing you've done that can't be undone. And as long as there's tomorrow, there's always hope. But you have to know that and to believe in yourself." Her cell phone interrupted with a Jamaican island tune, and after looking at the caller ID, her eyebrows came together in worry. She said, "I'll come back tomorrow at 11:00 AM. I won't be so easy on you next time," as she turned and quickly walked out.

As he watched her go, somewhere deep within he couldn't help but be pleased with her nicely shaped rear side. Even in the medical blues she looked good. But, pushing that thought quickly aside, he decided that he'd tell her tomorrow that he's in too much pain to work out, or something like that. He didn't want to hear any more of that sappy "don't worry, be happy" stuff.

When she showed up the next morning, she just looked at him with smiling eyes and beckoned him with her index finger. He didn't know why that made him move. Maybe it was because under any other circumstances, he'd have jumped at the chance to come to her when she called him like that. She helped him into the wheelchair and put on the new leg. As she rolled him into the elevator, she finally spoke. "An elderly man went for his annual checkup, and his wife was with him. When the doctor came in to the examination room, he told him he'd need a urine sample, a sperm sample, and a feces sample. The elderly man was hard of hearing, so he said to his wife, 'What did he say?' His wife responded, 'He wants to see your underpants.'" Michael was so surprised that he couldn't help but laugh out loud.

She worked with him four times a week, working up to forty minutes each session. She had him learn to use his left arm again, pick up objects, and use a knife and fork. In addition to the exercises, she massaged the muscles and moved the arm around, stretching them each time a little more, until it hurt. He learned his arm's strengths and limitations. He learned how to walk and move the new leg, and his overall strength improved.

With his physical strength improving and her nursing him mentally, the gloom that weighed down his spirit gradually lightened. Sometimes after she brought him back to the room she would sit for a few minutes more, seemingly really interested in his law school experience and the things that he wanted to do. He looked forward to their meetings and became curious about her. She met his parents a few times. Michael was surprised at how Kenisha and his parents seemed to bond. He discovered from his parents that Kenisha was a very religious person. It surprised Michael that they would come to know this, because his parents were not religious.

The conversations between Michael and Kenisha gradually moved from the task at hand to personal things about each other. They discovered that they shared similar outlooks on life, justice, and morals. Her values stemmed from religious beliefs, while his just seemed innate. He was curious about her religion. She was curious about law school and his career plans. He learned that her two-year-old daughter, Kisha, was the love of her life.

They were just finishing up a difficult session about six weeks into rehab when he asked, "How long have you been married?" He didn't know whether it was the question or something else that caused the almost imperceptible tensing of her neck and shoulders.

"About five years," she said without adding anything.

"What does your husband do?"

"He runs a truck company. They do a lot of work for the city."

"What's the company's name?" He didn't know why he felt the need to pursue this with her, but he was surprised at how she seemed to clam up.

"AAA Trucking."

"Oh yeah, I've heard of that company," Michael lied. "So what's your husband's name?"

She moved quickly as if to wrap up the session and this discussion. "Joe. Look, let's get you upstairs so you can rest that leg of yours. You know you've only got a couple more weeks before you're released."

"I know. And I'm ready to go, because you're going to kill me trying to make me stronger."

"Well, you're welcome! You know that you'll have more therapy after you're released."

"That's fine with me. Otherwise I'd miss you."

"I only work with inpatients."

"Oh, you'll make an exception for me, won't you?"

She laughed. "I wish I could, Michael, but it doesn't work that way."

"Well, maybe we could go to lunch or something sometime, just to keep in touch." He didn't realize how that might have sounded inappropriate.

As he thought about it later, he figured she just didn't want to dampen his spirit when she said, "Maybe."

Chapter 5

The angelic hosts in heaven had not seen this kind of continuous effort from the Opposers in quite some time, especially with two individuals such as Michael and Kenisha. They rejoiced with the Creator because they were able to help out each time the Opposers tried to intervene with these two humans. Michael's mother Sophie's attempt to abort him had been thwarted by a simple movement of the inspirited egg to a tiny place where it could not be sucked out. And Kenisha's mother's womb had been scarred and warped by a coat hanger abortion. Kenisha's mother, Essie Brown, was seduced and raped at age fourteen while living in a foster home, and in her poverty, pain, and fear, she felt there was no other alternative. The human's hypocritical logic had made it criminal to abort and at the same time shameful, difficult, and unwise to birth. Abortion cannot kill an angelic host, even if the embryo is already inspirited; hosts are never lost to the Creator except by their own will. The coat hanger that killed the embryo should have killed Essie, too. But the Creator's healing touch helped her through it. And the miracle of her being able to birth Kenisha four years later made her dedicated to both her daughter and to her church, all of which helped both Essie and Kenisha to become who the Creator needed them to be in the Plan. The angelic hosts constantly rejoice at how the Creator turns around even the worse things that humans go through for the Creator's own good purposes.

The Angels, always on guard, became aware of another attempt by the

Opposers under way against Kenisha. Danger! Two angelic spirits swished quickly to intervene in the earthly realm.

Girlfriends

Kenisha's cell phone sang the island tune. She pulled it out of her purse that was in the front passenger seat while she drove east on Ninety-fifth Street. "Hey, girl. Yeah, I'm on my way now. Sorry I'm late. I stopped to pick up a bottle of champagne for the birthday girl. Is she there yet? Okay, I'll be there in ten minutes. I'm really looking forward to this!" She looked down to shut the phone off, just for a second. When she looked back up again, she was approaching a cement mixer at a construction site on the right side of the street, with its rear protruding into her lane. She had seen it as she was talking but didn't realize how close she was to it. She started to slow when she saw a large truck coming right at her, moving too fast for the heavy traffic. There was no time to maneuver. She could move neither to the left nor to the right. Before she even had time to brake, the truck was on top of her, blowing its horn loudly. She knew there was not enough room for her to get through, and this accident was going to happen. She stepped on the brakes and braced, screaming "Jesus!"

Then she was through it. She was amazed and perplexed. She felt as though there had been a slip in time or space or something, because she couldn't figure out what happened. She slowed and pulled over to the side, looked in the rearview mirror, and saw the cement mixer still in the same position. Maybe there was more room than she thought, but she looked again at the traffic stopping at the mixer and she knew that wasn't true.

She sat for a few minutes until her heart came back to a regular beat and her hands stopped trembling. *How could that be?* As she sat there trying to calm down, she remembered hearing old Ms. Wiley testify at the church prayer meeting about how the angels got her out of an accident like that. She didn't believe it at the time. Could it be true? She felt as if angels must have done it, because there was no way she could have gotten through that. She shut her eyes and prayed out loud: "God, thank you for sending your angels to rescue me."

A while later she was at her friend's house. Connie greeted her warmly. "Ms. Kenisha Brown Cooper, as I live and breathe. I thought you were going to call and cancel, again. It's good to see you, come in, come in." Contrellus Jordan and her husband, Kevin, lived on the first floor and rented out the second and third floors of their spacious 1940s classic three-flat brick on South Shore, right off Jeffrey Boulevard near Sixty-seventh. The area had been through difficult times but had been making a comeback over the last ten years or so. Younger upwardly mobile blacks were moving in and renovating the older homes. Connie gave Kenisha a big hug and ushered her in. "Everybody else is already here."

Connie took Kenisha's coat and led her into the living room on the left of a long hallway that went from the foyer to the kitchen in the back. The rooms were spacious, with tall ceilings and hardwood floors with four-inch baseboards throughout. Mary, JoAnn, and Kasey, the birthday girl, were well into conversation while a favorite oldie, "Stop to Love" by Luther Vandross, made the atmosphere festive.

Connie directed Kenisha to the sofa and put a mimosa in her hand. Mary and JoAnn sat on the large L-shaped brown leather sofa facing the fireplace, while Kasey relaxed by the large bay window in a matching recliner. Over the fireplace was a large mirror with a two-inch wood floral-patterned frame. Connie and Kevin had painted this room a light peach color, which worked well with the natural wood floors and windowsills. Decorative African-themed throws, pictures, and art pieces, as well as many framed family photos scattered about made the room warm and inviting.

Connie and Kevin did all right for themselves and seemed to have it all. Kenisha always felt a little jealous at how well everything seemed to be going for them, but she never admitted that to her best friend.

"It's about time you got here. What's the matter, that husband of yours wouldn't let you loose?" JoAnn asked.

Kenisha put her mimosa on the large glass and wood coffee table in front of the sofa as she settled in. "Well, you know I had to take Kisha over to Mom's 'cause he had to work—again," she said lightly, shrugging her shoulders.

Mary piped in, "He must be real dedicated to that job to keep going in on the weekends, especially on a nice Saturday afternoon like this one. Uh-huh, work." She bent her forehead down and looked knowingly over her glasses as she smirked.

Kenisha didn't want to go there, not now. She looked directly at

Mary and said brusquely, "You know how busy he is. He runs the business and he has to be there to supervise the crew. I'm just glad Mom is there to let me off the hook every once in a while."

"Yeah." Mary let it alone. "You work hard, too. What would we do without our moms?"

JoAnn lifted up her glass. "Let's have a toast for our moms. I looked in the mirror the other day and my mom looked back at me."

Connie held up her glass, too, and said, "Mirror, mirror on the wall, we are our mothers after all." They broke out in laughter and drank and chattered on familiarly with much needed friendship and joy.

Kenisha was the last to leave, needing to get her head straight before she got back into the car to head home. As she walked with Kenisha to the door, Connie took her hand and said, "Nisha, what're you going to do about that no-good philandering son of a bitch you call your husband? You know he's still messing around with that whore in Uptown." She was tipsy and didn't hold anything back from her friend.

"Lay off it, Connie. To be honest, I don't really miss him when he's not around. I never know when he's going to go off, and I'm just tense when he's there."

"What do you mean 'go off'?" Connie stopped, stood directly in front of Kenisha, and put her hand on Kenisha's shoulder, her voice rising. "He never hit you, did he? If he hit you, girl, you need to get out of that. I'll kill him. Kevin will kill him. Don't lie to me. Has he hit you?" Connie's face, full of emotion, was only inches away, as if her close proximity could wrench the truth out of her friend.

"Chill, Connie." Kenisha brushed past her, moving toward the door. "No, he's never hit me." She stopped at the door and looked back at her friend. "Although one time I thought he really wanted to." She hesitated, her shoulders dropping as if they were tired of the weight. "He just goes off sometimes, yelling about this and that. Sometimes he just seems to be mad at nothing in particular, but I'm the one he takes it out on. I don't know what's going on with him most of the time anymore. We used to talk, but not anymore. Most of the time we don't have anything to say to each other." Her hands flew up in resignation. "But he's still good with Kisha. Bought her a swing set for her third birthday. He loves that child." She turned and opened the door.

Connie held the door for her friend. "Well, maybe you can get him to go to marriage counseling. I hear Reverend Summers is pretty good."

Kenisha turned back to her. "Yeah, I tried to raise that up to him and he just got madder. I'm thinking I might go myself, though, because I don't know what else to do. Divorce is just not in the picture for me. You know Pastor Rowland would put me off of the nurse's board, out of the choir, and probably out of the church if I divorced Joe."

Connie held Kenisha's hand again. "Nisha, he won't put you out of the church. Those hypocrites up there cheat on their own wives. But he sure would take you from leading the nurse's board. I'm telling you, if that bastard Joe hits you, you need to get rid of him so you and Kisha can have some peace."

"But Jesus doesn't want us to divorce. It's in the Bible, so I just couldn't do it. Listen, Connie, I've got to go." She pecked Connie on the cheek, turned, and rushed down the stairs. "I love you. Thanks for everything. Bye."

"Bye, Nisha. If you ever need a place to crash, Kevin and I are right here for you. That room in the back has your and Kisha's names on it." Connie stood and watched her friend until she was safely in the car before shutting the door.

Kenisha rushed out before she started crying. On the drive back, she couldn't help but remember how bright and clear she thought her future would be when she married Joe Cooper. She was twenty-six then and was working at Cook County Hospital, about a year before she started at the VA Hospital. Joe was six-four, with medium-dark brown skin. He had wavy hair, wore a mustache and had a dimple in the middle of his strong chin. He was handsome to most women. She talked herself into believing Joe was her soul mate, but somewhere inside she knew that he wasn't. He was her mom's first choice, not hers. She could hear her mother's voice even now, encouraging her to go out with him. "He goes to church and he's got a good job—he runs his own business! And he's so tall and handsome. What more could you want, Kenisha? You won't find anybody better than Joe."

Somehow Kenisha thought that when she fell in love there would be something more special about it, something that felt so real that she wouldn't have any doubts. But Joe fit neatly into all the right categories, and she couldn't come up with any reasons not to love him. When Kenisha tried to tell her mother she wasn't sure if Joe was the right one for her, Essie would have none of it. Essie was shorter and thinner than Kenisha. She seemed to need to make up for her smallness by the strength of her willpower. When Essie thought she was right, she would argue with her daughter until she wore her down.

Essie's words were etched into Kenisha's psyche: "You don't want to end up without a good man, Kenisha. I know. I was so scared when I had you all by myself, but I was so angry at everybody around me that I wouldn't let anybody into my life until Pastor Owens got through to me. I'm so glad I found the Lord when I did, because without God I never would've made it." Essie would look up at Kenisha with her left hand on her hip and shake her right index finger. "Nisha, baby, Joe's a good man, and you're not getting any younger. It's good you went to school so you can take care of yourself, but it would be better to have someone to share your dreams with, who you can build a home with and raise children the right way. You don't want to end up like me."

Kenisha's response was always to try to make her mother see that everything came out okay. "Mama, you raised me the right way. You did the best you could, and I love you for it. You brought me up in church, and I know right from wrong." She didn't know why her mom always put herself down. Kenisha thought the world of her mom for caring for her the way that she did.

Overcome by Essie's urgings and her girlfriends all thinking Joe was a slice of heaven, Kenisha finally caved in. She decided she was just being selfish and "living with her head in the clouds," like her friends were always telling her. So she just pushed that nagging little voice, the one inside that told her it wasn't all it should be, to a hidden place somewhere deep within. Now she couldn't help but ask herself whether she was any better off with Joe than her mother was without a man. She never felt more stuck in her life and didn't know where to turn. She buried herself in her child, her church, and her work, and she tried not to think too hard about it.

Chapter 6

The angelic hosts rejoiced as only they could do, which would have sounded to the created world like angelic choirs singing. They often rejoiced at what might seem like little things to the world—accidents that didn't happen, conversations that did. Sometimes they even rejoiced in times of stress and trouble to the children, because they could see a larger picture and knew at least some of the good things that could come out of the difficulties. What seemed like problems to the created children were often lessons from the Creator to teach and stretch them. Through difficulties, the children learned to deepen their compassion, their knowledge, and their search for truth, as well as their understanding of and faith in their Creator.

The angelic hosts know how difficult it is for the children to remember what they are to do in the world—most of the Angels have experienced creation themselves. They also know that as long as the children are somewhat faithful in how they use the gifts they take with them into the world, the Creator will make a way for their return. And so far Kenisha and Michael were both using their gifts for good purposes, as intended. These two were moving in the right direction, in spite of having forgotten so much.

Healing

"Hey, watch how you handle those boxes. That's important stuff there." Michael directed the maintenance crew as he struggled into his new office carrying a large potted plant. The boxes were mostly filled with books, pictures and office adornments, many of them graduation gifts from family and friends. When the maintenance crew left, he looked out the window of the small office to see the back of another high-rise building. *But it's a window,* he thought. *The view will have to come later. My first real job!* He flexed his hand reflectively as he thought back on his interview with the chief of the criminal division, Harvey Cutlett, in mid-January, just about one month ago. He had been released from the hospital about a year before, around the end of December 2002, and he was chomping at the bit to go to work.

"You've got good grades, Michael, and since I'm a Northwestern grad also, I know you had to work for them. I've learned that the best trial lawyers are not usually the ones with straight-A grades. The brightest students don't always know how to relate to the people in the jury boxes." Chief Cutlett clearly thought that was a compliment, but Michael wasn't sure quite how to take it. "What makes you want to work in criminal law, Michael?" Chief Cutlett asked.

"I'm hoping I can be involved in the fraud division, if that's possible, sir. I'm interested particularly in tax and computer fraud. You can see by my background that I took classes at the business school in accounting and finance, spent two summers clerking for Judge Myerson, and spent a lot of time doing research on abusive tax shelter cases. I'd like to stay in that kind of work."

Cutlett looked at Michael with unwavering clear, blue eyes as he leaned back on his chair and tapped his pencil. He carried his authority comfortably; that he was the boss was clear to Michael. "I read your résumé, Michael. It's impressive. With your background and your stint in the armed services, you'll probably get offers from a couple of the big firms. Why would you want to work for the U.S. Attorney's Office?"

This was a question Michael had asked himself more than once. He sat forward on the edge of his chair as he answered eagerly. "I'll be honest, sir. I really get a kick out of busting criminals, especially white-collar crime. It's just so wrong to see how some of these guys can get away with stealing and cheating while they feed off the public, and so many people are injured when that happens." His clear eyes were bright with sincerity as his brow frowned. "When the public trust is eroded by corruption, people feel the only way to be successful is to be more crooked than the next guy. I guess it sounds kind of idealistic, but I'd like to be one of the people who help to restore the public's trust in government and in honest business."

Cutlett grinned. Michael didn't know if he was laughing at him or with him.

Cutlett sat forward as he said, "You sound like a politician." That sounded cynical to Michael, until Cutlett went on. "But I like your idealism. We have a couple of openings in the Fraud Division, and I don't expect they'll be open for long. We could use you most in Frank Divine's unit. They've got a couple of big cases coming down the pike. The job is yours if you want it, starting in February."

Michael grinned too widely to look professional, and said, "I do, and thank you sir."

Michael grinned widely again as he thought back on that conversation. It was now Thursday, February 2, 2004, and he was starting his new job as an Assistant U.S. Attorney, Fraud Division, Chicago. Michael's reverie was interrupted when Frank Divine walked in the office to drop an armful of case files on Michael's desk. Divine was the manager of Unit 2 of the Fraud Division. Michael estimated him to be in his mid-fifties. He was starting to bald and struggling not to become overweight. He always wore a suit to work but generally took off the jacket soon after arriving and rolled up his sleeves. There was a frumpiness about him that made him comfortable to be around. Divine constantly chewed on a toothpick, which Michael figured was a sign that he used to smoke cigarettes.

"Here's some work to get started on," Divine said without stopping. "Read through the files and meet with me tomorrow at nine thirty sharp. Staff meeting is tomorrow at 4:00 PM. Welcome aboard." Then he walked out.

Michael spent most of the day reading through the files, getting organized in his office, and meeting with the other attorneys in the unit and with a couple of other new attorneys. His office was one of six in an office suite. The attorneys each had an office with a door that opened into a reception area where three secretaries and a couple of law clerks worked. After the suite emptied around 6:00 PM, Michael turned on his iPod and played some of his favorite oldies as he put books on his bookshelf. He liked music that his parents had played a lot when he was a boy, the Motown sounds, especially. He was singing off-key along with Smokey Robinson, "Baby, take a good look at my face. You'll see my smile looks out of place …" when Luellen, his latest "friend" called his cell phone. He had been dating her for about two months now.

"How about dinner at my place tonight, Michael?" Her voice lilted softly, as always. Her flirtatiousness had attracted him for a while, but right now it was irritating. He had begun to feel as if it was time to pull back before she thought this was something more than he thought it was. Michael was five-eleven, and other than his broad shoulders, he was slim. His hair was dark brown and slightly curly, and he wore it a little long, just enough to be almost radical but not quite. His eyes were light brown and unusually clear. It was difficult not to turn away when he focused intently on you; he seemed to look not just at you, but into you. He didn't have a huge sense of humor, but if you could get him in a light mood, he could be funny and fun to be around. He was twenty-eight years old, a war hero and a lawyer. His slight limp from the prosthesis seemed to add to his attractiveness to the ladies, which he fully enjoyed, until they wanted to hang onto him too long. Michael was happy that he didn't have to make up an excuse not to see Luellen tonight.

"I've got some work to do tonight." He was abrupt, and he knew that would bring about a pout, so rather than listening to her whine about not seeing enough of him, he quickly added, "But what about this weekend? We could catch *Pirates of the Caribbean* on Friday."

She said, "I hate to wait so long to see you. I miss you …"

He cut her off. "Got to go, babe, my boss is coming in the office." So he had to lie anyway.

Michael caught the brown line "L" back to his new apartment around 8:30 PM on a chilly, rainy late March evening. He moved into this apartment in a rehabbed six-flat building just north of Lincoln Park on Oakdale at the beginning of the month. The best thing about this neighborhood was its ample supply of restaurants and bars and things to do in general. He thought it was perfect for a single professional like him. He planned to get a Cubs season ticket one day, because the stadium and Wrigleyville were nearby.

On the way home he got off at Wellington to pick up some Thai carryout and walked the two blocks east through the rain, which was now a downpour. He broke into a trot but was still soaked by the time he got to his apartment. His leg began to throb as he carried his briefcase, laptop, and food up the front stairs and two flights up. He knew that he needed to call his doctor to see about this new pain but kept putting it off.

Michael's new position wasn't much on the Fed pay scale; starting at grade 11, he made a little less than $57,000. Even though that was scaled for Chicago, it wasn't enough to live really well in the city. After deductions, his take-home check every two weeks was less than $1,500. But $1,200 a month for the somewhat roomy one-bedroom apartment was considered a bargain in this popular neighborhood. He liked the shiny hardwood floors and in-building laundry, as well as the modern kitchen rehab and new kitchen appliances, even though he rarely used them.

Clothes, books, papers, and shoes were strewn around the large living area that abutted the kitchen. He hadn't gotten living room furniture yet, so a folding card table and four fairly unstable chairs served as his desk. The kitchen island countertop served as his dining table—usually he ate standing up and getting ready to go. On his bookshelf were mostly law books. The mantel held pictures of his family and some with him and his army buddies. His weight set stood in front of the bay windows that opened to a view of the tree-lined street with similar apartment buildings.

After dropping his things and getting into some dry clothes, Michael stood in front of the bay windows gazing reflectively as he ate dinner out of the carton. The bare trees emphasized the dreariness of this night—there was yet no sign of spring—but the dreary, dark evening put him in a meditative mood. It had taken him three weeks to get completely moved out of his parents' home in Lincolnwood. The year or so he spent there after his hospitalization was kind of amazing to him. He was there to watch his parents become involved in Temple Micah, a Reform synagogue near their home. They started attending regularly when he was still in the hospital, and they told him that their conversations with Kenisha got them started. She told them her faith kept her grounded while she worked with so many men and women with broken bodies at the VA.

His parents told him they felt lost as they struggled with seeing Michael's pain, and that his attitude toward them added to their difficulties. As he recalled their conversations, Michael still regretted how he, in his depression while in the hospital, had pushed them away repeatedly. His parents blamed each other at first, and tension between the two of them added to their pain. After leaving the hospital one day and not speaking to each other all evening, Jeffrey Lindebloom told his wife they needed to seek marital counseling if their marriage was to survive. That shook up Sophie, who agreed. Kenisha's conversation with them about her faith helped them to decide on going to a nearby local synagogue to see if they could get counseling from the rabbi there, who to their surprise was a lovely young woman. She was happy to meet with them and helped them to open up to each other with honesty and truth about feelings that had weighed them down for many years. That's when they started attending Sabbath services regularly.

His parents said that the music, the goodness of the people they met, and the helpful discussions with the rabbi kept drawing them back. The changes he saw in his parents over that year made Michael's heart sing. Michael watched how his mother worked at not being critical of his dad and how they seemed to really start talking to each other more, going out and having fun together. They became involved with other couples from the synagogue, going out to dinner and participating in activities there.

Michael knew that God's presence in his parents' lives had finally made life better for them. He attended services with them once and enjoyed it, but he didn't go back. Somewhere inside he knew what they were doing was right, but to him, participating in a synagogue just never seemed important enough to give time up for it. Isn't it good enough to God for him to try to be a good person?

As he mused in front of the window that cold rainy night, Michael realized that for the first time in his adult life, it felt good to be with his family. His job, his new apartment, the relationship with his parents and his family, and his newfound popularity all made him feel that life was good again. The only word he could conjure up to describe how he felt about life right now was that he felt "whole"—almost. And he didn't know what the "almost" was all about. Somewhere in a deep place, he knew there was still something missing, but he couldn't quite put words around what it was.

Chapter 7

The Opposers don't have power to inspirit embryos as do the angelic hosts; they can only wreak havoc among those already born. And that they do very well. When a creature's willpower is twisted and removed far enough from its original purpose, the Opposers can enter and take over the soul. The Opposers use fear, their best weapon, abundantly. Fear leads to lies and the desire for power over others. Fear ensures that the children's continual search for comfort is never satisfied, warping that natural need until it is turned into systemic greed. Greed is so ingrained in their world that the children do not even recognize it for what it is. Fear, lies, greed, and lust work well for the Opposers.

The two called Kenisha and Michael have proven difficult, so far, but there are always others around them. These two must be stopped.

Broken

"You look mighty nice in that nurse's uniform, Miss Kenisha," Deacon Oglethorp said as he took off his hat with a low bow and a lustful look. He thought it was okay to ogle all the women as they came out of church, and it really irritated Kenisha. Kenisha and Mary left the two-story, 1,000-seat sanctuary that took up most of the first and second floors of Deliverance Church on Martin Luther King Drive near Thirty-fifth Street. They headed toward the nursery that, along with the fellowship hall, took up the remaining space on the first floor.

Kenisha whispered to Mary, "How can that creepy old coot be a deacon?"

Mary laughed. "Yeah, he does it 'cause he knows some of those old ladies haven't had anybody to look at them like that in a long time, and they like it." They laughed as they walked down the hallway leading from the sanctuary to the fellowship hall and the nursery.

"What's so funny?" Pastor Keith Summers broke into their joke as he came from behind them. Pastor Keith was one of the associate pastors of the church, in charge of the Sunday school, the after-school programs for the kids, and the pastoral counseling center. He still had on his clerical robes because he served as worship leader, and he was probably going to the fellowship hall before heading to some meeting or visitation.

There was something about Pastor Keith that Kenisha really liked. The best way to describe him was medium: medium height, medium weight, and medium brown skin and eyes. He seemed sincere about his work. She wasn't sure why she liked him. Maybe it was his eyes. When she looked into them, she just felt that he was a good person to talk to. That's why she'd called him to make an appointment about her and Joe.

Kenisha responded, "Oh, hi, Reverend Summers." She turned to her friend. "Um, Mary, can I meet you in a few minutes? I need to talk to Reverend Summers about something." Kenisha knew Mary would be okay with that.

"Hey, I've got to go anyway. Mark's waiting for his dinner. I'll call you later. Take care, Reverend Summers." Mary gave her a hug and him a smile and went down the hall toward the nursery.

Pastor Keith smiled. "I got your message but didn't have a chance to call you back before service today. What's up?" he said lightly.

"Do you have time to talk to me? I mean, I've been looking for someone to talk to about … a problem," she said hesitantly. There were people all around, and she didn't want anyone to know that she was scheduling a counseling session with Pastor Keith.

His smile turned into a gentle frown of concern. "Sure, Kenisha, how about on Tuesday? That's April 20, isn't it? I'm in the office in the afternoon."

She reacted to his concern by trying not to seem desperate. "I get off at three, but I don't have to pick Kisha up until about five. Can I come at three-thirty?"

"Three-thirty's fine. Do you want to let me know what it's about?" he said quietly.

"It's about me and Joe," she said softly. "I'd like for him to come, too, but I don't think he will."

She saw the compassion in his eyes and heard it in his voice. "If you can get him to come, that will be good. But if you can't, you just make sure you come, anyway, hear? And no matter what, you know that everything is going to be all right, don't you? You know that God is always with you, especially in the tough times." He looked right into her eyes and smiled again as he spoke softly.

That should have made her feel better, and it did help, but the relief was coming through as tears that she didn't want him to see.

"Okay, Reverend Summers, I'll be there." And she rushed off, down the hall to the nursery to pick up Kisha and then out to the parking lot. It was raining. Not enough to open an umbrella, but dripping just enough to be felt. That's how she felt inside, like she was dripping while trying to hold back the imminent emotional downpour. She put Kisha into the child seat and got into the driver's seat. Then she couldn't hold the tears back anymore. She was miserable because Joe hadn't come home again last night. "How did I get myself into this mess? How can God be with me when life is so hard?" she said softly to herself as the tears flowed. She involuntarily let out a sob as she lowered her head onto the steering wheel.

"Why are you crying, Mommy?" Kisha asked with a wavering voice that preceded a cry. The bright and active three-year-old was reacting to her mother's tears sympathetically with her own. Her curly hair was pulled into two small ponytails with pink ribbons at the top and bottom of each. The curly, fine hairs that wouldn't stay in the ribbons lined the edge of her face like a halo.

Kisha's voice made Kenisha try to pull it together. She turned to looked at Kisha before she started the car. "It's okay, baby. I just had something in my eye. I'm not really crying." But the tears were still on her face.

"Don't be sad, Mommy." Kisha continued to frown into a cry.

"Don't worry, Kisha, everything's all right. It's okay now." Kenisha's voice was soothing. Then she said brightly, "Didn't you learn in Sunday school that God is always with you?"

Needing to change the subject, she turned back toward the front and looked at Kisha through the rearview mirror. "What did you do today in the nursery?"

"We made paper angels. See?" Kisha held up a cutout white paper angel colored with crayon strokes of pink, red, and yellow.

"Yes baby, I see. That's a beautiful angel." She put the car in gear, turned on the windshield wipers, and headed home.

The house was a spacious yellow brick traditional Chicago bungalow, near Ninety-third and Damen in the Beverly neighborhood. The brown awning on the front, a new brown slate roof, and large front yard gave the home a pleasant curb appeal. Joe and Kenisha had moved there about four years ago, when she was pregnant with Kisha. They chose the home because it was in a well-maintained upper middle-class, mostly African American neighborhood. Kenisha also liked the fact that the house was not far from her mother's home, a straight shot east down Ninety-fifth Street to Ninety-seventh and Prairie.

Kenisha parked the car in the garage and walked with Kisha up the stone walkway to the side door that was the main entryway to the house. A large living room with bay windows and a fireplace was to the right of the entry. To the left was the dining room, which had been recently remodeled so that it flowed into the updated kitchen, divided by a kitchen island. Behind the kitchen area were cabinets and a breakfast nook that opened through sliding glass doors onto a large deck and backyard.

Joe came in just as Kenisha was sitting Kisha down at the table in the breakfast nook for her lunch. "Daddy!" Kisha shrieked with joy.

He scooped her up in his arms. "Hi, baby. My, you look so pretty! Give me a kiss." He kissed her and tickled her at the same time.

Joe had a way of lighting up any room he entered with a bright smile and a hearty laugh. Kenisha had learned the hard way that the smile that he shared with the public only came into the house when they had visitors.

Joe sat Kisha back down to eat and went up to the bedroom without a word to Kenisha. Kenisha went upstairs a while later and put Kisha down for her nap. She went into their bedroom where Joe was sitting on the bed reading the newspaper. He would be on the offensive, she knew, because he was in the wrong. He had this way of attacking her verbally as an offense mechanism—it kept her from complaining. In her head were all the words that would share how she felt: the heartbreak, the confusion, the anger. The words in her head were: *How can you treat me like this? Who is she? Why can't we talk about it like adults?* But she knew that if she spoke these words, if she tried to get him to converse about what was going on with them, he would respond by attacking her viciously, and he would somehow end up saying it was her fault. He wouldn't let up until she either got crazier than he was, which was always dangerous, or until she walked out of the house. Nothing would be resolved by trying to talk to him or telling him how she felt when she knew he wanted to fight.

Kenisha went to the dresser and started moving things around, straightening up, as Joe ignored her. The movements helped her nerves as she thought about how to get him in a good enough mood to talk about getting counseling. After a few moments, she said, intentionally calm, "Want some dinner?"

All that accomplished was to send his antenna up.

"No, I ate already," he responded moodily, shaking and then turning the page of the paper.

She began changing her clothes, trying to think about something that would change the charged mood of the moment. "You should've heard Pastor Rowland preach today. He was on fire." The minute she said it, she knew it was the wrong thing to say.

"Well, why would I want to do that? Somebody needs to turn some fire on him. I don't know why all you 'Christians' give your money to that man. That's all he's after, money, and I don't trust him any further than I can throw him. Hmmmph, on fire. Shit, one of these days, he'll be on fire for real." He popped the paper as he turned the page again.

She took off her nurse's whites and put on some blue jeans and a yellow T-shirt, one of her favorite things to wear. She tried to ignore his irritation. "I saw Reverend Summers after church. You know him, Keith Summers? He was in your high school class. He's moving up in the church, heading up the after-school program and the counseling center."

"Oh yeah?" He responded intentionally with an inflection that told her that he didn't want to talk about it.

Before she could think of some other way to bring up counseling, he got up abruptly, left the bedroom, and headed down the stairs to the family room. They had refurbished the large room on the lower level of the home with comfortable leather furniture, a large-screen television, and a fireplace. She knew he went down there to watch sports on the fifty-six-inch high-definition television. He chose not to be in her presence when he knew she wanted to talk, and that was most of the time lately.

When he left the room, Kenisha sat on the bed with pillows at her back, pulled out a pen and her journal from the nightstand drawer and began to register her frustration in writing. She'd been keeping the journal off and on for the past five years or so, at the suggestion of one of the Bible study leaders. It was supposed to help her spiritual walk, but it lately had turned into a way of recording heartbreaks. She didn't know how that would help her spiritually, but it helped to release her feelings.

She read through a few of the older accounts, like when she was so excited about being back in church. When she started going to college, her attendance at this church that she grew up in became sporadic. She started going regularly again right after college, when she first started working as a therapist. She met Joe at church, and up until a few years ago he used to go with her somewhat often.

She never imagined her marriage would have turned out like this, and tears started to well up again as she read her entries. Her mother and her friends encouraged her to date Joe, even when she was not sure about him. He looked good, had graduated from the University of Illinois, was making a lot of money with his own business, and even though he wasn't at church every Sunday, he attended often and was on the trustee board. He seemed ideal, at least to her mom, but there was something about him that just didn't sit right with Kenisha. She couldn't put words around it, though.

Kenisha put down the pen and rested her head back on the pillows, while she let her mind wander back to how she ended up marrying Joe. They had dated for only a few months before he asked her to marry him. She thought he was still seeing other women, and they hadn't had sex yet. Even more, they hadn't had intimate conversations very often, even though he'd been quite attentive and they talked about a lot of things. They didn't really talk about how they felt about each other very much. In a way that was good, because she didn't really know how she felt about him. She put off answering him, but over the next month or so he continued to ask, claiming he was in love with her and telling everybody they knew that he wanted her to be his wife.

Her mother was the one who pushed her. She knew that her mom had had a rough time, having her as a teenager before she graduated from high school. Kenisha knew her mother's story well. Essie made it a point to be open with her only daughter about her life. Kenisha figured Essie was trying to make sure that Kenisha didn't have to go through what she went through, and it seemed to work. Kenisha didn't rebel as some of her friends did with their parents.

Essie's mom had raised her alone, working as a house cleaner until her dad was released from prison when she was nine. The next three years Essie didn't talk about, except to say that her no-good father got her mother hooked on crack, and then they both tried to turn her out to do tricks. She was on the street when the cops picked her up and put her in the children's home when she was twelve years old. She told Kenisha she was really okay with being there, until one of the counselors took a liking to her when she was fourteen, told her he loved her, and got her pregnant. Abortions were illegal at the time, so he took her to a hack who used a coat hanger in her. While it did kill the fetus, it almost killed her, too.

Essie told Kenisha that she went through a period of sexual excesses after that, for reasons she could not explain to either Kenisha or herself. Essie was in the middle of her senior year, still living in the foster home, and almost eighteen when she found herself pregnant again. She never told Kenisha who her father was. Kenisha wondered if she even knew. They said it was a miracle Essie was able to birth Kenisha because her womb was so scarred.

Essie was all alone when Kenisha was born, and it was a difficult birth. Essie thought she would be on welfare, but it was the Deliverance Church's ministry to teenage moms that helped her make it. Through the people in that ministry Essie found strength, the help she needed with her self-esteem through counseling, and the loving care of the pastor and his wife, who let her live with them and helped her to care for Kenisha while Essie went back to finish high school. Essie was able to get a job as a receptionist at a local government agency, which translated later into administrative assistant. She became able to take care of her child by herself and even bought a little bungalow near Ninety-seventh and Prairie when Kenisha was fifteen.

Essie was now fifty years old to Kenisha's thirty-two, had never married, and was determined to live out the life she never had through her daughter. Somewhere deep inside, Kenisha felt that her mother blamed her for being born.

After musing about her and her mother's lives for about thirty minutes, Kenisha began to pick up around the bedroom. She spent the rest of the afternoon and evening cooking, ironing and straightening up around the house. After her nap, Kisha went downstairs and spent some time with her dad and her toys. Kenisha did not say anything more to Joe, other than to have him send Kisha up for her dinner around six. She knew he would stay downstairs the rest of the evening, into the night, falling asleep until late morning.

After getting Kisha bathed and in bed, Kenisha prepared her clothes so that she could be ready to leave at 6:00 AM to take Kisha to the day care and get to work by seven. Around 9:00 PM, she vegged out in front of the television in their bedroom, too tired to think anymore. But even in her not thinking, her brain raced with questions, cries, and pain, and her mind automatically worked out plans to deal with it all. She'd just have to see Pastor Keith alone. That might be better anyway, she thought, but she wasn't sure why and didn't try to figure it out.

Chapter 8

These two are both young spirits, but the angelic hosts know they are strong. Some of the Angels have been in and out of the world many times. The more experienced they are when they come into the world, the more their earthly bodies seem older and wiser than their ages. The less experienced angelic spirits seem younger in their worldly bodies than their ages. But younger or older, they all forget who they are. While the older spirits are better equipped to bring early wisdom in the created ones, they can also find it more difficult to move in the new directions the Creator intends for them to go. The younger spirits are more flexible, but it is more difficult for them to remember who they are. If they are able to remember, they can help to make great strides, moving out of the limiting boundaries that the children always put on themselves.

That is what the Creator expects of Kenisha and Michael. The angelic forces continue to sing songs of strength and encouragement to them.

A Good Day

It was Monday, April 19, 2004. Michael would remember this day for the rest of his life. He got to work early, at 7:00 AM, because he was going to take a few rare hours off during the day to go to the VA to fit a new prosthesis. The night before, his leg had pained him again. Michael's doctor told him the recurring leg throb came from a slight crack in the prosthesis and that he needed to get a new one. He put it off, not wanting to take the time off work. He already had missed two appointments to get the new one fitted, but the pain wouldn't let him delay any longer.

It was damp, windy, and a chilly forty-five degrees, cool even for Chicago in mid-April. Michael left the office at eleven fifteen for the eleven-thirty appointment, hailing a cab in the front of his building on Dearborn to take him to Damen Street, right off the Eisenhower Expressway, which should be about a ten-minute ride. His leg was throbbing when he got into the taxi, and he was happy that he'd be able to finally get this done. As the taxi turned off Dearborn toward the Eisenhower, Michael couldn't help but think about Kenisha, wondering if she still worked there.

Traffic in the Loop was jammed up unbelievably. The taxi was only able to inch through. At about eleven twenty-five they were almost at the Eisenhower, so Michael thought he'd be a little late but not too bad. Damen was one of the first exits from downtown. But no sooner than they got on the expressway, the traffic stopped again, to a complete halt. They inched forward at an excruciatingly slow pace.

"I can't believe this! What the hell's the problem now?" Michael's blood pressure was rising as fast as they were going slow.

"Don't know. Accident, weather?" the East Indian driver calmly responded with a heavy accent.

By the time they pulled off on Damen and into the hospital driveway, it was a little after noon. Michael made it downstairs to rehab, only to find his doctor had left for lunch already.

"Relax, Mr. Lindebloom." The receptionist tried to calm Michael down. "Tony will be back between one and one thirty. Lucky for you, his one-thirty appointment just called and cancelled, if you can wait." She smiled as if there was nothing for him to be upset about. "You can have a seat, if you'd like to wait here."

"Yeah, right, lucky for me," Michael muttered to himself. He looked around the bare-boned waiting room with orange plastic furniture and some old *National Geographic* magazines and health reports from the hospital scattered around to occupy the patients as they waited. His mood was foul now, and the idea of sitting there for one and a half hours didn't help. But he really didn't want to put off getting this new leg.

"I'll get some lunch," he told the receptionist, as he walked away mumbling to himself about having to waste so much time.

He remembered the food in the cafeteria as not half-bad, so he thought he'd pick up a *Sun-Times* and catch up on the news while he ate. He found a newspaper kiosk right outside the elevator doorway near the cafeteria and put in a quarter, but nothing came out. He shook it but nothing happened. He lifted his fist in rage to bang it one good time when he heard her voice in his ear.

"It costs fifty cents now."

He turned and there she was, looking beautiful as ever. His rage melted away into a helpless grin, just like that.

"There you are, right when I need you, again," he said.

Kenisha smiled. "What're you doing here? Don't they have any decent food downtown?"

"Need a new leg fitted. Appointment … late … look, can we catch up? I'd love to have lunch with you."

Kenisha was still smiling. "Sure, Michael, I was hoping you'd say that."

He ordered a hamburger with grilled onions and mushrooms, fries, and a Coke. She got a tuna fish on rye with chips and lemonade.

She was through the line first and navigated to a table for two over by the wall. As Michael came over to sit down, he wasn't sure what to say first. "So, what's happening in your world?" Always a good opener, he thought.

"Everything is going well. How have you been, Michael? The last time I saw you, you were looking for a job. What're you doing now?" Kenisha leaned forward, smiling as she opened her chips.

He smiled back. He was happy she took over the conversation. "I'm working with the Feds, at the U.S. Attorney's Office over on Dearborn Street. They've got me in the fraud and corruption branch. Fun stuff, huh?"

"I can see how fraud and corruption would be fun for you." She laughed.

He guffawed a lot louder than appropriate. "Well, you're right about that. Unfortunately, the only thing I get to do now is read a lot about it in the briefings and write legal briefs about it. Maybe I should be on the other side."

"I'm just kidding, Michael." She said his name a lot. "I bet you're good at your job." She took a bite of her sandwich.

"I want to be. There's something about people who rip off others that just rubs me the wrong way," he said sincerely. "Hey, you've changed your hair. It used to be blonde. I like it dark, too." It was dark brown now, straight and long. He figured it was her natural color, but no longer styled naturally.

"Thanks for noticing. I just decided that blondes don't have to have all the fun."

He guffawed again. He wondered, while he was laughing, what it was about her that made him act so goofy. Was she intentionally teasing him? "Well, it looks nice. I like it. So, how's Kisha? She's what, three now?"

"Kisha's three, going on thirty." She laughed again. "She's fine. She's a real blessing to me."

Michael thought he saw something in her eyes but wasn't sure what it was. "It sounds like you're doing pretty good. Life is good for you, isn't it?" There it was again, he was sure, something in her that was a little sad—in her eyes, but only briefly. He bit his burger.

"Everything's okay," Kenisha said. "Joe's doing well with his trucking business, my mom's doing great, and church keeps me busy when I'm not here. My life is full. How's your family, your brothers?" She took another bite of her sandwich and waited for him to answer.

Michael chewed and swallowed before speaking. "They're doing well. Charlie's had a new baby since I was here last, makes three. And Jonathan got promoted on his job and moved to Schaumburg. I think Dad's feeling the best right now, since I'm working and on my own. I'm the last one he'll have to worry about." Michael suddenly sat forward with an excited gleam in his eyes. "Oh, I wanted to tell you that you really had an impact on them."

Kenisha looked surprised. "On who?"

"My mom and dad."

"Really?" Kenisha's eyebrows went up, questioning.

"Yes." Michael continued to lean forward. "Really. You said something to them about having faith in God when I was in the hospital, didn't you?"

"I probably did." Kenisha didn't let on whether she remembered or not.

"Well, Mom and Dad decided to go to the synagogue to talk to the rabbi and ask for prayers because of what you said to them. The rabbi told them they should come to the synagogue and pray for me. They went and were so moved that they've started going regularly. And the amazing thing to me is that they've really changed. They get along so much better now than they did before. It's really great!" Michael finally sat back.

Kenisha smiled broadly. "Oh, Michael, that makes me feel so good. I don't even remember what I said to them. But I'm really happy for them."

"Look, Dad's retiring next month. Why don't you and Joe come to his retirement party? It's going to be casual, a backyard barbecue, on June 19. They'd love to see you again." Michael took another bite of his hamburger to give her time to respond.

Kenisha took her time answering. She felt a little awkward about sitting alone with Michael, even though she had selected the table. Everybody knew she was married. But she'd eaten with patients before. She didn't really know why this felt so awkward. All she really wanted was to talk with him, to see how he was doing. But why she felt good around him, why he made her feel a little nervous and happy at the same time, she didn't know. Somewhere in the back of her mind—a little deeper than the spoken thoughts, but not so deep that she couldn't feel them—she felt a spiritual connection. But any further ideas about the two of them were cut off by the reality of her world. He was a patient whom she liked, and that was all.

The thought of going to a party up in Lincolnwood where she wouldn't know but a few people, and none of them very well, didn't sound like much fun to her. She knew that Joe wouldn't come. Besides, she didn't know Michael that well. He was just a patient whom she liked to talk to, that was all.

"I don't think so, Michael. Joe's awful busy almost every weekend these days." Joe sounded like a good excuse to her.

"So? If Joe is busy, you can come and bring Kisha. We'd love to meet her, too. I'd really like for you to come. I promise you'll have a good time."

How can he promise that, when my life is in tatters? she thought. She didn't want to go, but she decided to be gracious. "I don't think so, but who knows? Send me a note with the details, and I'll think about it. Here's my e-mail." She wrote it on a napkin.

"I'll put your name on the invitation list. Please try to come. It would mean a lot to me." Michael returned to his hamburger.

Kenisha couldn't help but wonder whether he just wanted to have somebody black at the party so that people would be impressed by how liberal his family was. But then she stopped herself. She didn't really know him well enough to think that, either. Or did she? *There's something about him that I like, so I ought not to judge,* she thought.

"I'll try," she responded without commitment. She really didn't want to tell him no, but she had no intention of going to his mother's home. "So tell me about these big important criminal cases you're working on, if you can."

Michael continued to eat as he talked. "Most of the work is boring—going over documents, drafting legal briefs. I don't think you'd find that very interesting. Except in one case, which you've probably read about in the newspapers. I've just been assigned to help out on the trucking scandal case. You know, there was a big accident downstate, and people were killed by a drunken truck driver who didn't have a valid license."

"So where's the fraud in that?" she asked, thoughtfully.

"The reason he didn't have a valid license is that his company was paying off somebody in the government to keep them from checking into the background of their drivers. And the thing about it is that it looks like it might go a lot higher up than anybody realized when the case first started."

"How high up? You mean the mayor's office?" she asked calmly, but her mind went on red alert. Joe's trucking business had city contracts, based on him being a minority business owner.

"No, the city government's not involved in this one. It's all the state of Illinois. And I can't tell you any more than that. You'll hear more about it in the news pretty soon, though."

She breathed a sigh of relief. "You get 'em, tiger. I watched how tough you fought to get out of the hospital when you were here. I know you're going to be a great lawyer."

Michael laughed. "There you go again, cheerleading."

She went back to eating, embarrassed. "I just believe you can do it, that's all."

"I didn't mean that in a negative way. I really enjoyed our time together when I was rehabbing, and your encouragement helped me to want to get well. When I first got here, I didn't think I would have a life. You changed all that," he said sincerely.

"Oh please." Kenisha didn't know how to respond. She was uncomfortable with his compliments. She sat straight up and looked at her watch. "Oh my. Look at the time. What time is your appointment?" She was all businesslike now.

Michael looked at his watch, too. It was just about one thirty. "Yikes. I've got to run. But about the party, please come? I'll send you an e-mail with the address. And if you're downtown anytime, stop by the office. I'd like to show you where I work. Maybe we can have lunch?"

"You better go before you're late. It was good seeing you, Michael." She was up and away before he could say anything else.

Michael thought he had overdone it with Kenisha and kicked himself mentally, quite soundly. He finished the last of his hamburger before taking his tray. *What's wrong with me?* he wondered as he put the napkin with her email address in his pocket and walked to the elevator.

Chapter 9

What the Opposers hate most, and fear most, is the earthly creatures' ability to truly love. True love, that selfless and caring compassion for others, wreaks much havoc on the Opposers' plans. The Opposers go to great lengths to confuse the creatures' desire for sexual pleasure with that kind of true love. They want to keep the creatures from understanding the great power of love that cares more for others than self. When the creatures don't remember, they don't understand that they are made from love for love, and they don't understand the power of love as a weapon against hate, fear, greed, and all that the Opposers stand for.

Yes, there have been times when one of the creatures learns to wield the mighty power of selfless love greatly against the Opposers. When that happens, the creatures honor them as heroes. But few are strong and brave enough to do that.

Opportunity

"Another stack of files for you to go through." Frank Divine dropped the stack on Michael's desk, disregarding the files already there. "We've got to move on this. Word is that the newspaper is going to publish the details before we get the indictments filed. This one's going all the way to the top. These are notes recorded from meetings with John Bergman, Secretary of State. I need you to go through them and highlight any inconsistencies based on the tapes from the phone taps. And check to see if there are any inconsistencies with the interviews with the head of the licensing department. How're you doing with the immunity brief?" Divine chewed nervously on the toothpick out the side of his mouth as he spoke.

"It's done. June is putting it in final form now. Do you want to take it up to the top?" Michael leaned back on his seat.

"That's where it's going whether I want to take it there or not. We've got a briefing with Cutlett at 4:00 PM next Monday, April 26. I want you there in case he has any questions about the details of the phone taps. Make sure you bone up on them before we meet. Anything else?" Divine was brief and to the point, as always, leaving Michael feeling as if there wasn't enough time for anything else.

Michael shook his head. "No, not now."

"You're doing a good job, Michael. Keep up the good work." When Divine turned and went out, the air seemed to suck out of the room with him.

Michael was excited about being involved in such a high-profile case so early in his career. He knew that if this case reached the governor's office, it would be big. There were some in his office who were not happy about him working on this case, particularly Julia Dressen, who worked in the same office suite with him. She had been there four years and was stuck with trying a couple of minor tax fraud cases. Divine said she had her hands full and gave this one to Michael against her protests.

Michael almost lived in the office some weeks, even staying overnight to finish the briefs early a couple of times. Julia was married with two kids and couldn't get away with that. Michael thought that it wasn't really fair to her, because she was a good attorney and had paid her dues. But he lived on this stuff and, besides, his commitment to this work gave him a good excuse when he didn't want to be bothered with females. He needed them when he wanted them, and needed an excuse when he didn't want them around.

Luellen hadn't lasted very long. He simply said to her that he needed to see other women. She couldn't handle that and dropped off the scene. There was Wendy after that, and he also dated Vicky for a while at the same time. His aloofness made him a challenge to women, and the aggressive ones put him in their scopes and usually got to him first. That was okay with him. He didn't want to work too hard at it.

He thought that he might find someone who would make him really care, but he didn't want to worry about it.

A few minutes after Divine left, Julia stuck her head in his door. "Hey, Michael, how about lunch?" She was somewhere between thirty-five and forty-five, Michael guessed, with medium-length dyed-blonde hair, small eyes, and a mouth slightly too big for her face. She always wore pantsuits, usually black, gray, or navy blue. Today's was gray.

He was surprised that she would ask him to lunch. She didn't go to lunch very often, and when she did, she usually went out with a couple of her attorney-classmates in the Civil Division. He looked at his watch: twelve forty-five. He hadn't even thought of eating, but for some reason he felt this might be an opportunity to get to know her, and he was hungry now that he thought about it. "Okay, give me until one o'clock?"

"Sure," she said. "Just come to my office when you're ready."

When he came to her door a few minutes later, he said, "Can we go someplace quick? Divine just gave me a big load with a deadline this afternoon."

"Sure, Michael. I just got a new case, too, so I need to get to it." Julia obviously wanted him to know about her new assignment.

The sun was shining brilliantly on this late April day, and a warm, gentle breeze off the lake invited all those cooped up in the stacked high-rise cubicles out to lunch. The streets were crowded as Michael and Julia navigated their way to hunt for food. They ended up in a nearby soup, bread, and salad restaurant and chatted nonchalantly about family and office stuff while they waited in the crowded line. There was nowhere to sit, and they felt lucky to find a spot at a tall but tiny table, intended for people to eat standing so that they would move on quickly. As they began to eat, he asked what he knew she wanted him to ask: "So tell me about your new case."

She looked at him and smiled. "Can you believe that the city has its own trucking scandal?"

"Really?" Michael was surprised that the city of Chicago would have a trucking scandal at the same time that he was working on one involving the state of Illinois. "Any connection to the state case?"

"Not this one. It looks like the city transportation department has been taking bribes for trucking contracts. We're not sure how high up it goes yet, but it's nice and juicy." Julia licked her lips as she ate her salad, seeming to enjoy that there was corruption.

"Who are the targets?" Michael was really interested in this because he thought there might somehow be a link to the persons involved in the state case.

"Well, it's not all clear just yet. The FBI is trying to get wires on a couple of truck company owners. The rumor is that organized crime may be behind it."

"Sounds exciting." Michael was impressed and happy for her. "Look, Julia, I know that you didn't want me to be assigned to the state case, but I want you to know that I really admire your work. I think the chief just wanted somebody who he could work day and night on this one. I'm glad you've got a plum case." He wanted to be friends with her, because he really did like her.

Julia stopped eating and looked at him for a moment before responding, as if she was evaluating whether he meant what he said. "Yeah, I never know how to keep quiet when somebody's stabbing me in the back. But I don't really blame you, Michael. It's Divine who made that decision. I wanted to have lunch with you to let you know that I don't blame you, now that I can see straight again." Julia seemed sincere.

"Okay with me. I could use a friend around the table when Divine is raking me over." Michael wanted her to like him, too.

"Yeah, he can be a real shithead, can't he?" They laughed and started to talk about office gossip.

Chapter 10

The angelic chorus sang songs of comfort and support to Kenisha. How cruel the Opposers can be. And how easily they worked through people in all walks of life. It wasn't just Kenisha's husband who could stop her from accomplishing her role in the Plan. Her religious training was also a big problem for her. Even the children's efforts to worship the Creator are not immune to the fear and desire for power that the Opposers wield so well. The children's belief systems are riddled with their own rules and regulations—some made up by misguided ones from a lack of understanding. And too often the rules and regulations that become traditions are created for selfish purposes.

Blessed Assurance

She was early for the three-thirty appointment. The secretary, Vanessa Clark, was friendly. Too friendly. It was like she rehearsed being super nice because she worked in a church.

"Good afternoon. How can I help you?" Her voice was syrupy sweet, and she smiled, but it didn't feel like a friendly smile.

Kenisha took it as a personal put-down, but she didn't know why. She had never met Ms. Clark before but had seen her around church. "I'm a little early. I'm Kenisha Cooper. I have a three-thirty appointment with Reverend Summers."

"Oh." Her smile faded into an expression of concern. She looked at the clock. It was 3:17. "Pastor Keith isn't here yet. I'm sure he's on his way. Why don't you have a seat, sweetie. Is there anything I can get you?" She nodded her red pressed and tightly curled head toward the leather couch by the wall. Vanessa Clark looked young to Kenisha, maybe thirty or so. She wore heavy make-up and had long designer fingernails.

Something about all that she said and did just rubbed Kenisha the wrong way. Both her friendliness and her concern felt like they were an act to prove to those who came into this office that she was most holy. But underneath it there was something else, something you didn't want to touch. Kenisha almost asked for a drink of water, though she knew Ms. Clark would have resented that. Kenisha decided to be nice and do what was expected. "No, thank you. I'm fine."

She didn't want to engage in mental battle with Ms. Clark. She had more important things on her mind. She was surprised how well the day had gone. She was able to take off a little early for a change, and the blue line "L" was right there when she got to it. She took it to the Loop and transferred at Jackson Street to the red line that brought her to Thirty-fifth Street, about a ten-minute ride from the Loop. Then, the bus was right there at the train station, to take her the few blocks east to the church, which is between Thirty-fifth and Thirty-sixth streets on Martin Luther King Drive.

She liked to think that making all of those connections was a sign that she was doing the right thing. Kenisha was feeling anxious but hopeful about this conversation. All she wanted was to be able to talk to somebody who could help her work through her feelings and give her some help in dealing with a husband she didn't understand.

Pastor Keith came in at about three twenty-five, and Kenisha jumped up to greet him before he reached Ms. Clark's desk. "Hi, Reverend Summers, I got here early."

"Hi, Kenisha." His smile seemed genuine. "Let me get settled, and I'll be right with you." Kenisha sat back down.

Vanessa handed him some pink telephone messages. "Mr. Curry called again. And Pastor Rowland said there's a ministers' staff meeting tomorrow at 9:00 AM." She didn't really need to tell him what she was handing him. It made her seem more important, as if she had some power given to her in all of this.

"Thanks, Vanessa. I'll put it down." He went into his office and shut the door.

He came out a few minutes later after having relieved himself of his jacket and briefcase, as well as the phone messages, and escorted Kenisha into the office. "Vanessa, will you hold my calls?"

"Yes, Pastor Keith." She said with another syrupy sweet smile, and then she looked at Kenisha with feigned concern, again.

"Have a seat, please, Kenisha." Pastor Keith moved around to his seat and allowed her to choose which of the side chairs she wanted. She sat directly across from him, not on the closer chair that was on the right of the desk.

The office felt pleasant to her. It was small, about ten by ten. Just enough room for an average-sized desk and two side chairs, a credenza behind him, and a small computer table on the left side of the desk. Two bookshelves were hung on the right wall, and on the left, a coat rack stood next to two windows looking out over the parking lot behind the church. Behind him were his degrees from Hampton University and Howard Divinity School, his Certificate of Ordination, and a couple of certificates, one from the city of Chicago for participating in the "Hope Project" and another from the Sunday school in recognition of his leadership.

She hung her purse on the chair's arm and leaned forward, nervously. "How are you today?" she asked, trying to remember to be gracious.

"It's been a busy day for me. It seems like there's more work than time these days." He smiled at her. "How has your day been?"

"It went well today, Reverend Summers—"

He interrupted her. "Look, everybody around here calls me Pastor Keith. I wish you would, too."

"Okay," she said. "I managed to get off work on time for a change, and the train was right there when I got to the blue line, and so were the red line and the bus at Thirty-fifth Street, so I made it here without any problems." She looked down at her hands in her lap. "I wanted Joe to come with me, but I couldn't get him to talk about it." She looked back up at him. Pastor Keith sat straight, with his hands folded neatly on the desk in front of him. He seemed relaxed and open, somehow empathizing just by being there.

"That's okay, Kenisha. It's perfectly fine just to have you come in." His voice was soothing. "Let me say before anything else that everything you say to me in this time of counseling will be held in strict confidence. I won't share your information with anyone else. And you should also know that I'm a pastoral counselor, not licensed as a professional therapist. I can talk to you about personal and marital problems and about your spiritual life. If it seems that you have needs that are beyond my training, I'll let you know that and refer you to someone who may be of more help. Is that okay with you?"

"I guess so. I'm here for help with my marriage. I just don't know what to do." She started to tear up again and reached for a tissue from a box that was strategically placed on the outer corner of his desk, away from the papers and books that were mixed up with pictures of his wife and three children, miscellaneous office utensils, and the large calendar in the middle over which he worked.

He leaned back, crossed his legs, and waited until she was ready to speak again. "What's going on?" he asked casually, with a slight frown of concern. He did not emote with her, and his relaxed and patient demeanor helped her pull it together.

She blew her nose and sniffed. "We don't really have a marriage anymore. Joe and I hardly talk. He always seems angry at me, and I don't know what I've done." She paused there. She didn't know how much to tell Pastor Keith. She didn't really want him to think too badly of Joe, who was a church member, after all. She gently rubbed her nose again with the tissue.

"How long have you felt this way?" he gently prodded.

"It seems to be getting worse these last few months," she replied. "To the point that we never have any real conversations. Before then, we got along okay as long as I didn't do anything to upset him. We've been married for over five years now, and to be honest, I'd have to say that things changed not too long after we got married. Especially after Kisha was born, and she's three now. He just seemed to get …" She struggled for the right word. "… mean." She said softly, with her head down, "He just seems to hate me."

"I'm asking this to help me understand the depth of your problem, Kenisha. Is there any physical abuse?" he probed gently.

She looked up and said, "No, no. He's never hit me. But he's been angry enough that I thought he might, just last week."

"Tell me about that." Pastor Keith continued to tactfully and professionally get her to detail her concerns about her relationship with Joe. They continued to talk until about four fifteen, when Pastor Keith began to sum up the session. "I see why you're troubled, Kenisha. I'm glad that you're here, and I surely would like to continue to meet with you to help you see your way through this." He became quiet for a moment, looking out the window. Then he turned to her and asked, "Which Bible class do you attend on Sundays?"

"Deacon Tyler's," she responded.

"Hmmmm." He was quiet again for a bit, as if he was trying to decide something. He finally spoke again. "Has the class discussed things like divorce?"

"Yes. I know that Jesus doesn't want anyone to get a divorce and that women should let the men be the head of the household. I know that, Pastor Keith, and I want to do what is right. That's one of the reasons I came here, because I want to be obedient." She didn't know how to say to him how trapped all that made her feel.

"I thought so. We don't have time to go into it deeply today, but let me say to you briefly that when Jesus said that 'anyone who divorces and marries another is committing adultery,' he was talking mainly to the men. In those days, only men in the Jewish faith had the right to divorce women; women didn't have that right. The reason Jesus said what he did was because the men were abusing the women, divorcing them just by giving them a piece of paper for little or no reason. That left the women without anyone to help them. They didn't work outside their homes, weren't educated, and often weren't accepted back into their own families. Jesus was upset with that. Jesus also would not want anyone to live in an abusive situation. His teachings on divorce have to be understood in context.

"We can talk about this more later, if you want. Please understand, I'm not encouraging you to get divorced. I believe that you ought to stay together for the family, for the children, as long as it is possible and in the best interest of all. But if that doesn't seem possible, you need to know that divorce is not completely ruled out. But let me say again, I don't believe that's true in your case. We'll do our best to help your marriage become healthy again.

"Kenisha, I want you to know that more than anything else, God wants all his children to be safe and cared for. God is love, and God wouldn't mandate that any of his children live in a situation where they are abused or hurt. You must know that God loves you, even in your pain. Your job is to do your best to see if you can work it out, and you're doing the right thing by getting help. We'll talk next week some more about how you can maybe help get Joe back into church and into counseling. But in the meantime, the most important thing for you is to know that God is your shepherd, who will lead you to places of peace and comfort, who will protect you from evil, and who wants you to have joy in this life."

He opened his Bible, turned to the 23rd Psalm, and read it to her slowly and with feeling. "The Lord is my Shepherd, I shall not want. He makes me lie down in green pastures. He leads me beside the still waters. He restores my soul …."

"It's a wonderful psalm, isn't it?" he asked when he finished reading.

She nodded, tears welling up again.

"The reason this psalm is so comforting is because it reminds us that God is always with us, caring for us as a shepherd who loves his sheep, even when we're going through difficult times. And it reminds us that God only wants what's best for us." He looked right into her eyes, and she felt the depth of compassion in them.

"Do you have a daily time for meditation and prayer?" he asked.

"I say my prayers every night, and I study the lesson for Bible study, most times. Oh, and I have a journal that I write in sometimes." She didn't want to lie to Pastor Keith; she wasn't really regular in her personal Bible study time.

"I'd like to meet with you again next week, but I want you to do this for yourself in the meantime. I'd like for you to read the 23rd Psalm every morning this next week. Read it and take your time with it, pausing to think about what the psalm is saying to you. Then take a few minutes to jot down some notes about it. It will help you get through each day with more peace. Will you do that?"

"Yes, Pastor Keith." She thought that would be good. She already was thinking about getting up fifteen minutes earlier and working that into her schedule.

"Would you like to pray with me before you go?"

"Yes. Thank you, Pastor Keith. I feel better already." She did. Inside she felt as if a burden had been lifted from her heart, even though nothing had really changed in her life—just her way of looking at it. After they prayed, she thanked him again, and she left to pick up Kisha with real joy in her heart. She really liked Pastor Keith. He seemed like the real thing.

Kenisha thought a lot about what Pastor Keith said about divorce. She had never heard that before. She didn't want to do anything to violate God's laws, and she really didn't want a divorce, especially for Kisha's sake. But somehow, just knowing it could be a possibility helped her to feel less trapped.

After Kenisha left, Keith sat and thought sadly about her situation. He was convinced that she suffered from mental abuse, the kind that could escalate into physical abuse. He had seen it too often. This woman was loved by so many at the church. They saw her good side, the caring person who worked as a nurse on Sundays to help if anyone became ill during the worship service. The seniors especially loved her, and that made him know that she had a good heart. He knew that she wasn't perfect. No one is. But he also felt she was telling the truth, and his heart went out to her in her pain. Why would her husband treat her so shabbily?

Keith didn't know Joe very well in high school. They ran in different circles. Joe was popular and athletic, Keith was neither. In church, Keith interacted with Joe mainly through some of the board meetings he attended, mostly business meetings about property and finance. Joe hadn't been around for a while, but when he was, he liked to use his wealth as a bludgeon to get the board members to do what he wanted. Keith thought Reverend Rowland gave Joe too much deference. But the church always needed money, and Joe made a lot of money with his business, so everyone thought he must be pretty smart. And he did contribute generously to the church from time to time.

Keith realized he would likely only have Kenisha to work with, but vowed to himself to help her. He liked her spirit.

Chapter 11

Anger raged among the Opposers. Another powerful weapon against them was courage that is driven by love. Kenisha's understanding of love was more than most. If she began to remember and to exercise her gifts fully, she'd grow beyond the simplistic teachings and limitations the Opposers had been able to use so deftly with so many others in the world. And Michael's courage and willpower were stronger than most. If he remembered and found his direction, he'd be a force to contend with.

Trouble

Michael stood in the door of Julia's office and stretched. "Hey, Julia, I don't know about you, but I need a break. My eyes are crossed from reading. How about some lunch?" Her office was always neat, as if she cleaned up every day. She had brought in a small decorative throw rug and a desk lamp. Family pictures and a few art pieces sat among her law books on the bookshelves. A shawl adorned the back of her desk chair. Her office said she was relaxed and a tastefully organized person.

She looked up with glasses perched on the end of her nose. "I wish I could get away, but I've got a transcript to go through before we go to Judge Keystone for another phone tap this afternoon. Will you pick me up a sandwich from the deli, please?" She had been working almost exclusively on this new fraud case for the past two months, stressed by her superiors and the fear of impending publicity to move it as quickly as possible.

"What kind?"

"Turkey with mustard, no mayo, and a diet Coke. And one of those chocolate chip cookies. Here, let me give you the money now." She pulled open the bottom right-hand drawer and took out her purse.

"So what's happening in your truck scandal world?" Michael asked as he stepped in her door. It had been a couple of months since they'd talked about it, other than brief reports at staff meetings.

"Well, we're trying to get a phone tap on the chief of the transportation department. I'm sure we've got enough info from this taped conversation to warrant the order. We want to see just how high up this thing goes." She opened her wallet and pulled out a ten-dollar bill and two singles.

"You think the mayor's in on it?" Michael was intrigued.

"I'm not sure. It is possible. And the possibility of an organized crime connection is pretty clear, too. It's not just bribes, we know now. There's some phony fronting in the minority-owned businesses, too. We had one of the company owners talking, and he implicated about seven other ones. But he disappeared. I don't know what happened, but he could be hiding out from the mob." She hesitated. "Or worse. I can't help but wonder if somebody's leaking information." She handed the money over to Michael, across the desk.

Michael asked, "What companies?"

Julia sat back and hesitated before she answered, as if wondering why he'd ask that. "I don't think you would recognize them by names. Vito Garreli is the one who was talking to us. He owns Sta-Safe Trucking. Been running it for ten years and sending bribes to the transportation department for at least the last five years. We have a taped conversation between him and Mark Garoway, who's the go-between taking the money to Jon Cunningham in Transportation. We think he's the organized crime connection, but we're not sure. The other ones we're sure about are Safety Trucking, Marita's Trucking, and AAA Trucking. That one's on the south side, supposedly a minority-owned business, but we think it's a front for somebody else. We're not sure who. What's his name—Joe Cooper, a big shot on the south side who likes to hobnob with Chicago's finest."

"Hey, sounds like you've got them cold." Michael suppressed his surprise at hearing Joe's name, put Julia's money into his jacket pocket, and left. He should have thought of it before. That was Kenisha's husband. Michael struggled with how to deal with this new information. He knew he shouldn't share information about an ongoing investigation with anyone, especially a potential target. If he told Kenisha, she would tell Joe, who could alert all of the rest of the potential targets and abort further fruitful investigation. He picked up a couple of sandwiches, took Julia hers, went back into his office, and shut the door.

He couldn't help himself. He would hate to see Kenisha and her family hurt by this. He knew that if Joe turned himself in and shared information that implicated someone higher up, he would likely be able to get out of any serious criminal charges. And that would be good for both the investigation and for Kenisha and Kisha. The problem was that he couldn't be sure how Joe would respond.

His hands shook as he dialed the number of the VA rehab unit. He asked when his next appointment was, which he knew wasn't for a couple of months. He tried to sound nonchalant when he asked how he could reach Kenisha Cooper. The receptionist told him she was in Unit 3A and would connect him.

When Kenisha picked up, he said, "Hey, Kenisha. This is Michael Lindebloom."

"Hi, Michael." Her voice sounded happy to hear from him.

His mind pictured her smiling. "I need to talk to you," he said soberly.

"Well, here I am. What's up?"

Kenisha sounded so carefree. He hated to give her bad news. "I can't talk to you about it over the phone. Look, my dad's retirement party is tomorrow evening. You got the invitation, didn't you?" Michael tried not to sound too worried.

"My, my, sounds intriguing. But I really can't make the party tomorrow. I don't have anyone to watch Kisha, and Joe's busy."

Michael knew she was brushing him off, and that hurt. "Look, Kenisha, this is important." Michael was whispering now. "It's about your husband and his business. Remember where I work?"

Kenisha's voice registered both surprise and concern. "Oh. I see. Yes, well, I'll try to come. What's the address again? Wait a second, let me get a pen to write with." She paused for a moment and then said, "Okay."

"It's 4652 West North Shore Avenue, Lincolnwood. Five o'clock. Come up the Eden's Expressway. You have to stay to the right and take 94 where it splits off from the Kennedy. Then exit at Touhy, going east. Make a right onto Cicero at the exit, go about three blocks, and then make a left on North Shore." Michael couldn't figure out how to keep her from worrying when there really was so much for her to worry about.

Chapter 12

It is both amusing and sad to the hosts that all the children's various religious groups think their limited insights are more correct than all the others, as though any of them truly could know the full mind of the Creator! Not even the hosts have that knowledge. The children's misguided desire for power and control, coupled with such a limited ability to understand, infects all that they do and has the consequence of separating them from each other. When they battle against each other over religious beliefs instead of focusing on the true battle between good and evil, their religions become neutralized and inconsequential.

If Kenisha and Michael can remember well enough who they are and what they are to do, they will have the child who will push forward the Creator's Plan greatly. The angelic hosts keep close watch over both of them.

Dismay

Kenisha hung up the phone, went to her locker, and nervously put the address in her purse. She wouldn't have any problem with Joe; he wouldn't be home anyway. She'd ask her mom to watch Kisha for her. She found herself unable to concentrate for the rest of the afternoon and worried in her head all evening. It was Friday. She'd have to make it through the rest of this evening. *The Lord is my Shepherd* … Just the thought of the 23rd Psalm comforted her.

That evening, she only saw Joe for a few minutes when he came in around eleven o'clock and went downstairs to watch television. She didn't want to talk to him until she knew what this was all about, but she had her suspicions. She thought of all the worst possibilities, and high among them was Joe's arrest and her having to raise Kisha alone, amid the publicity and the pain of public humiliation. She stopped herself and tried to remember the 23rd Psalm again. She repeated softly as much as she could remember: "The Lord is my Shepherd, I shall not want. He maketh me to lie down in green pastures. He leadeth me beside the still waters. He restoreth my soul … Yea though I walk through the valley of the shadow of death, I shall fear no evil, for thou art with me. Thy rod and thy staff, they comfort me …"

Saturday morning, she studied the psalm and found herself repeating "He leadeth me beside the still waters" over and over, until she felt some measure of calmness. Joe left around 10:00 AM, right after he got up. She went through her Saturday events: the nurses association meeting, of which she was treasurer, getting groceries, and then taking Kisha on a "playdate" with her friend down the street. At about 3:00 PM, she gave Kisha a snack and went upstairs to try to figure out what to wear. It was a barbecue, but she knew she should not dress too casually. She remembered Michael's mom as very chic, even when she was visiting him in the hospital. She chose a matching set of casual pants and knit top, a lime green.

She got into the car at about four thirty to first drop Kisha off at her mom's house. Essie had offered to keep Kisha overnight and to bring her to church in the morning, which would be a big help. She hadn't really lied to her mom when she told her she was going to a barbecue up on the north side at a friend's house who she met at work. Essie didn't ask for a lot of details. She was probably happy to see Kenisha getting out for a change.

Kenisha stopped by a drug store near Ninety-fifth and MLK Drive to get a card. She didn't have time to worry about a gift and hoped the card would suffice. She didn't want to be early or even on time. She figured she'd get there at around five thirty. She wanted as little attention as possible. She planned to stay just long enough to find out what Michael was talking about.

As she directed the car back west on Ninety-fifth Street over to the Dan Ryan Expressway, the oldie "My Girl" by the Temptations was playing, but her worry wouldn't let her sing along. As she headed north on the Dan Ryan, traffic became heavier just before she entered the downtown area, but not heavy enough to slow it down. She maneuvered over to the left middle lane on the four-lane highway to avoid the slowest traffic. Cars were merging onto the expressway from downtown Chicago on the left while others were moving over from the right, angling to get into the express lanes, which were on the left, a little past the downtown area.

Right after the express exit, the lane on her left merged into her lane with little warning. Kenisha looked to her right and attempted to move over to avoid the merging cars, but she couldn't because there were two large semis next to her on the right and one directly behind her as well. And traffic was still too heavy and moving fast. As she turned back, she saw a black convertible sports car speeding up along her left, disregarding the merging lanes. There was no room to maneuver. She couldn't slow down, she couldn't speed up, and she couldn't move out of the way. She held tightly onto the wheel and braced for the collision. She screamed.

Nothing happened. For the second time in just a few months, she felt something that she could only describe as a blip in time, a moment that just seemed not to be there. It was as if she was somehow fast-forwarded to another space in time. She was amazed that the black convertible somehow ended up in front of her, when it didn't seem possible. *Am I losing my mind?* she wondered as she said a prayer of thanksgiving and cursed the other car's driver at the same time. The traffic seemed to suddenly lighten, and she was able to move into the center lane and slow down a bit. A gospel tune, "That Name" by Yolanda Adams, came on:

This name speaks peace, unto my storm clouds,
This name speaks calm, unto me fears.
And when I feel that no one loves me,
His loving presence is so near.

She sang along, trying not to tear up.

As she exited the Edens Expressway and approached Michael's father's house, her mind raced with what she should say. She couldn't imagine Michael's parents understanding why she was there. She had

had some pleasant conversations with them when Michael was in the hospital, but she didn't feel like a friend of the family.

The home was a 1950s split-level in a neighborhood of the same. The yards were generous in size, trees lined the street, and flower gardens were abundant. *This is a well-cared for neighborhood,* Kenisha thought as she parked the car. The aroma of meat grilling welcomed her as she walked to the front door. She nervously rang the doorbell. She rang it again after about twenty seconds, wondering if anyone was in the house or whether they were all in the back.

A young woman who looked to be in her mid-twenties answered the door. She had dark hair, curly and short. She was petite, no more than five-two, with three-inch red sandals, an orange, red, and yellow flowered flowing skirt, and a red tube top, showing more than a little cleavage. Kenisha was glad she hadn't put on the blue jeans that she started to wear.

"May I help you?" the young lady asked in a high-pitched but raspy voice.

"I'm Kenisha Cooper. Michael invited me to the party."

The woman raised a plucked and filled-in eyebrow. "Oh, really? Come in. Everyone's in the backyard. I was getting some drinks in the kitchen when I heard the door. I'm Katlyn Garner, a friend of Michael's. How does Michael know you?"

Kenisha knew that was the question Katlyn wanted to ask most of all, and bristled. "We've known each other for a while." She told herself to be nice. "It's nice to meet you. Which way is the backyard?"

"Follow me." Katlyn headed straight through the living room to the kitchen. "Would you be a sweetie and carry that pitcher of lemonade for me?" Katlyn picked up a large, plastic-covered bowl as she nodded toward a pitcher on the kitchen counter.

Be nice, Kenisha told herself again as she picked up the pitcher.

Katlyn smiled as she led Kenisha through the kitchen and out the back French doors that opened onto a wooden deck.

The backyard scene was pleasant. There were people on the deck, under umbrellaed tables and laying out in deck chairs. The large yard ran back about fifty yards, with two large oaks on either side of the back fence. The grill was in the middle of the yard, with a couple of small tables near the grill and three longer tables nearby lined up with all kinds of food. There were two picnic tables, several folding chairs, and a couple of blankets on the lawn. A wide array of annuals (petunias, fuchsia, and hibiscus were the only ones that Kenisha could remember by name) defined the yard on both sides, and there were hosta in the corners. In the middle, a bed of roses.

Kenisha estimated about fifty or so people, and she was surprised that they included quite a cultural mix. Her fear of standing out as the only black person was swiftly put away, as she was able to see six or eight black folks, a few Hispanics, and an Asian couple in the mix. To make it even better, the CD player on the deck was playing "I Hear a Symphony" by the Supremes.

As Kenisha stood at the doorway to the deck, Katlyn went down into the yard and put a possessive hand around Michael's waist, breaking into his conversation with an older couple sitting in lawn chairs. Michael turned quickly and, escaping from Katlyn's arm, seemed to bound up the deck steps.

"Kenisha, I'm glad you could make it." He leaned toward her, as if he would hug her, but seemed to think better of that and reached out his hand. She wrapped the pitcher of lemonade in her left arm and shook his hand. He really did look good, wearing some faded blue jeans and a T-shirt with a peace symbol on it.

He took the pitcher of lemonade from her with one hand and held her elbow with the other as he directed her down the steps. "My parents are over there. I told them you were coming. They'll be happy to see you. Did you find your way okay?" He seemed eager to please her. His smile said "relax."

She felt better about being there but could not relax. "Yes, the traffic was heavy for a while, but I made it okay."

Katlyn, looking on with one hand on her hip, came over to them as he brought Kenisha to his parents.

"Mom, Dad, you remember Kenisha Cooper?"

Jeff Lindebloom turned from his grilling, with a spatula in hand. "Yes, of course." His smile was genuine.

He looked older than Kenisha remembered, almost completely gray, with bags under his eyes. But his smile was broad, and his eyes twinkled. She hadn't seen much of that when Michael was in the hospital.

He put down the spatula and came over to her, holding out both his hands to her. She let him take her hands in his.

He said, "How are you? It's great you could come. Michael tells us that he sees you every once in a while when he goes over to the hospital for treatment. Young lady, I want you to know that you are welcome here. We are so grateful to you for how you helped our son come through that horrible tragedy." He seemed genuinely happy to see her.

"Yes, Kenisha. Welcome." Sophie Lindebloom had been standing near a table by the grill. She didn't look a day older. As a matter of fact, she seemed younger now, less made up and more relaxed than she was when Michael was in the hospital. She came over with drink in hand and gave Kenisha a hug.

"It's good to see you again, and we do thank you so much for all you did for Michael." She started to tear up but worked to control it. "You were wonderful. What would we have done without you? Charlie, Jonathan, look who's here!" she called out to Michael's brothers. "Here, have a seat. What can I get you to eat? How about a drink?" Sophie was so much friendlier and relaxed now that Michael was okay.

So much for not attracting attention to myself, Kenisha thought. Katlyn put another protective arm around Michael's waist as Kenisha became the center of attention when Charlie and Jonathan came over with their wives. This time, Michael put his arm around Katlyn's shoulders.

Aha, Kenisha thought, eyeing them as she sat down. She let Sophie make her a plate—a hamburger, some baked beans, and grilled vegetables. She ate and chatted with Sophie, Jeff, and several others who came to find out who she was. Several of them were Jeff's former staff members, friends from work, and neighbors. It was a friendly conversation and fun, but all Kenisha really wanted to do was to talk to Michael.

After she finished eating and chatting for what seemed a really long time, she asked for the restroom. Michael said he'd show her where it was, and escaping from Katlyn's grip again, he led her back into the house.

"I'm so glad you came," he said as they entered the kitchen.

"Michael, please tell me what's going on." Her eyes were full of concern.

He turned to face her, pursed his lips, and sighed before speaking. "One of the attorneys in my office is working on a hired truck case, the one involving the transportation department in the city. She told me that your husband's company is a target. This is serious, Kenisha." He looked right into her eyes as if he was searching for something there.

"Well, what … I" She struggled for some response as her mind grappled with the significance of what he was saying. "I thought you said the scandal didn't involve the city government."

Michael's tone was calming. "This is a different scandal, Kenisha. This one is about city contracts and payoffs and minority set-aside violations."

Kenisha felt as if her worst fears were coming true. "I don't know what to do. Do you want me to tell him, or what? I don't know anything about his company. He never talks to me about it." She paused as she realized she was assuming the worst. "He could be innocent," she said weakly.

"Look, Kenisha, I could get fired for telling you this. The FBI has been secretly recording conversations in Chicago's transportation department, and Joe's name has come up. If he's innocent, he should be okay. But if he's caught up in this thing—and there are a lot of companies that are—he could do serious time at worst. At best, he would be involved in ugly publicity that could ruin the business." He paused for a second to let that soak in. "Look, I've been thinking about it, and I think if we could get Joe to come in as a witness, we could save him from the worst of it."

"You want me to talk to him?" Kenisha was still trying to get a grip on all of this.

"Yes. He needs to go to the FBI or, better yet, the Assistant U.S. Attorney—her name is Julia Dressen—before they find out what they need from somebody else, and that's going to happen soon if he doesn't act now. I can't be involved. You've got to talk him into cooperating."

"I don't know if he'll listen to me, but I'll try. I don't want you to get into trouble over this. I'll figure it out. Thanks, Michael. You really didn't have to do this." Kenisha was grateful and amazed that Michael would put his job on the line for her, and she struggled with her heartbreak at the same time. For one of the few times in her life, she was at a loss for words. Just then Katlyn came into the kitchen to get her lock back on Michael. Kenisha went back out to say good-byes and made it back home.

Chapter 13

The Angels sang strength and comfort. Oh, how cruel the children can be when they are lost! How their souls can be corrupted and turned from the love and care with which they were created! The Creator weeps with them each time they hurt each other. The angelic hosts sang down songs of strength and compassion, because they knew the most difficult struggles were yet to come.

Pain

Kenisha arrived home at about eight thirty on Saturday, June 19, a night she would never forget. She was grateful that her mother was keeping Kisha overnight. How would she bring up the subject to Joe, who hadn't told her a thing about his company in years? How could she let him know that she knew about the scandal? He'd want to know where her information came from, and she couldn't tell him that.

She put her keys and purse on the table in the front entry and went downstairs to make herself a drink. In the cabinet over the bar were the makings for an appletini—just what she needed. A martini glass was already in the freezer. Joe must have put it in there for himself. She replaced that one, put two measures of Grey Goose vodka and sour apple schnapps with a little apple juice and a touch of Midori in the martini mixer with plenty of ice, shook it for about thirty seconds, and poured a drink into the cold glass. That was good.

She decided to sit there and try to think through her dilemma. About halfway through her drink, the only answer she had was a swirl of angry thoughts that wouldn't get her anywhere. She noticed Saturday's newspaper on the coffee table and picked it up. There, on the front page, was a teaser about the hired truck scandal. She didn't even know that the scandal was out yet. Why didn't Michael tell her that? She quickly read about how trucks that were supposed to be working for the city were sitting idle, while the owners of the truck companies were paid large sums of money in city contracts. The government officials were accepting bribes to give these contracts to the truck companies that did nothing. The focus of the news article was on a government official who headed the city's hired truck program.

Joe's company wasn't in there. With a sigh of relief, she thought this would give her what she needed to open the discussion with him. She finished her drink, poured another, and took a few sips when she heard Joe come in and go upstairs. It was about ten o'clock, early for him. She decided to take her drink and the newspaper with her to talk to him.

He was changing clothes, getting ready to go back out. When he saw her standing in the door, without stopping he said, "It's a party for one of the guys who works for me. I need to be there, to show my support." He buttoned his shirt and looked at her with eyes that said *don't start.* "Where's Kisha?"

"She's spending the night at Mom's." She didn't want him to ask why, so she said, "I just saw this news article about some bribery in the trucking business. Do you know anything about it?" She came into the room and stood near the bed, turning to face him as he stood dressing himself next to the dresser, in front of the full-length mirror on the closet door.

He put his tie around his neck, expertly working it around and, beginning to tie the knot, he took his time to answer with deliberation. "Not really. I know the guy in the transportation department, but I'm not involved with that. Why do you ask?"

He didn't sound intimidating, probably because he was feeling guilty about going out, again, she thought. She decided to keep at it, trying not to slur her words. She was surprised at how tipsy she was, so she sat down on the edge of the bed. "I was just wondering. I think if you know something it would probably be a good idea to tell somebody, to keep clean, you know." She hesitated. "Maybe you could end up getting more business."

"Since when are you interested in my business?" He seemed aggravated now, as he slammed the dresser drawer shut and went to the closet for his jacket.

"I've always been interested, Joe. I just thought of you when I read the paper and wanted to make sure everything was okay." She was beginning to sound whiny, even to herself.

"Well, don't you worry about me. I'll be okay. You don't have to worry about yourself, either. That's all you're concerned about." He looked at her and sneered. "You won't lose your fancy lifestyle, your nice home, your fancy furniture, and your car. You don't have to worry about going shopping anytime you want and spending all my money. You're just used to having everything you want. That's what's bugging you. You're not worried about me. You just want to make sure that you won't have to give up your lifestyle!" The more he talked, the angrier he got.

He pulled a jacket out of the closet, slamming the door. As he put the jacket on, he moved to stand over her as she sat on the bed. "I work my ass off so that you can live in luxury, and you come in here and tell me you're worried about me in some bribe scheme? Ha!" He stuffed his arm angrily in the jacket as he loomed over her, huffing, waiting for a response.

"I wasn't thinking about me, Joe." She tried to keep her voice calm, but she was not really in control. She stood abruptly to face him, still a little tipsy and spilling the drink still in her hand. He was forced to take a couple of steps back, but he still loomed over her. She had to look up to face him this close. "I really was thinking about you. Why do you always have to attack me every time I try to talk to you?" Her voice started to rise. "Why can't we talk like two adults? Why are you so angry with me? What did I ever do to you to deserve the way you treat me?" The liquor was taking over now. Everything she had been holding in her heart started pouring out, lubricated and dislodged by the alcohol. She faced up, trying to look at him eye to eye, with the martini glass wavering in her right hand.

Her voice went up an octave. "You think I don't know where you're going? You think I don't know about that bitch you've been seeing? Everybody knows about it. You think I'm a damned fool, don't you?

Well, you can take your black ass over to her house and stay there, you bastard. And don't you ever come back. I don't need anything from you! I don't want you in this house." She wanted to throw the drink in his face, but in a brief moment of sanity, opted instead to throw the whole glass against the closet door. The drink splattered over the dresser and the carpet as the glass burst into shards.

His face contorted with anger. There was something truly evil in the face that stared into hers, and it frightened her more than ever before. "So what, you crazy bitch! I paid for this house and everything in it. You think you're going to throw me out?" He grabbed the front of her shirt and hit her hard with his fist on the left side of her face, repeating "crazy bitch" and hitting her again and again. When she drooped unconscious, he let her shirt go, and she fell back across the bed.

She woke up about a half hour later, and he was gone. She laid there and cried, both for the pain in her face and the pain in her heart, big loud weepy sobs and moans. Somewhere in the back of her head she thought, *This is what the word "blubbering" means.* She got up after a while, went to the bathroom, and looked at her face. She was black and blue all over the left side. Her eye was swollen shut. Her nose was bleeding, and her lips were purple and swollen. She blubbered again as she ran cold water over a washcloth and started to dab at the blood. She cleaned up the best she could, took a couple of Tylenol PM painkillers, took off her outer clothes, and curled up in her underwear under the covers. As she fell asleep, the main thing on her mind was how to hide her face from her mother.

Chapter 14

Life in the created world is a temporary state, an existence that lasts only for so long as the Creator desires. True life, existence that is not limited by time or space, is only in the realm of the Creator. The earthly children who deepen their remembrance of the Creator know that all of the pain and sorrow they experience, even the worst things that happen, are only temporary. Without this understanding, the children have great difficulty coping with the evil, death, and destruction that are an integral part of life in their realm.

The Angels know that their work is complemented by the community of believers. How important it is for the children to help each other understand and to remember who they are! When they do that, they become each other's Angels all around.

Love Is All Around

Kenisha awoke a little before 11:00 AM to her phone ringing. It was Mom. She let it go into voice mail and listened as her mom left the message: "Kenisha, where are you? Mary says you're supposed to be on nurses' duty today. I took Kisha down to the nursery and I'm singing in the choir today. You know it's Father's Day. Do you know if Joe's coming to church? I can't pick Kisha up after church because I'm going out with Delia and Margaret to brunch. Where are you?" She was clearly irritated.

Kenisha knew she had to get up, but she lay there for a long time, thinking about what had happened. She was trying to help Joe, and as has been his pattern over the past few years, he attacked her. But she never thought he would hit her. Her mind kept replaying the evil she saw in his face, filled with so much anger and rage, all focused on her. For the first time, she faced the idea that she should get a divorce.

There was no love left for her in this marriage, if there ever was any. She felt she couldn't be the best mom to Kisha if this kept up. How could she raise her child to learn to love in a loveless marriage? How could she raise a happy and healthy child when she was always worrying and sad—and afraid? It became quite clear to her that she didn't want to raise a child in an abusive home. She knew her mom would have a fit if she left Joe, but her girlfriends would be happy for her. She thought she'd probably have to leave the church, and that would be hard, too. She reasoned she didn't need to stay in that house, either. A small apartment big enough for her and Kisha would be just fine with her. She didn't want to fight with Joe. She just wanted out.

She dragged herself out of bed, put on her favorite old terry cloth bathrobe and slippers, and wobbled down the stairs one step at a time to the kitchen. She took two extra-strength Tylenol, got some ice out of the freezer, wrapped it in a clean dishcloth, and held the ice against her face with her left hand as she clumsily made coffee with her right hand. She saw on the kitchen clock above the sink that it was a little after one o'clock. Church would just be getting out.

As she poured her cup of coffee, she heard her cell phone ringing from her purse in the entry hall. She put the cup down, got the phone, and looked at the caller ID. She knew she couldn't put her mother off any longer. She tried to sound normal as she answered. "Hi, Mom."

"Kenisha, where are you? Are you all right?" Essie's voice was pitched high with concern.

"I'm home. Mom …" She couldn't hold it. When she tried to talk to her mother, she started blubbering again.

"Kenisha, what's wrong? I'll cancel brunch, pick up Kisha, and be right over." Essie hung up, without giving Kenisha time to respond.

Kenisha sat down at the table in the breakfast nook, put her head in her folded arms, and cried.

When Kenisha heard Essie using her key to come in the front, she retrieved the ice pack, putting it again to the left side of her face.

Kisha, running, came in the kitchen first. "Hi, Mommy. Look what I made in church." She excitedly held out her newest paper angel before she looked up at Kenisha's face. Kisha's joy was immediately swept away. "Mommy, what's the matter? You hurt your face?"

"Yes, baby," Kenisha said softly as she continued to hold the ice to the left side of her face, hoping to cover as much of the damage as possible. "That's why I didn't come to church today. I fell down and hurt myself." She would never want Kisha to know what really happened.

"Does it hurt?" Kisha came over to grab her legs and hug her, eyes welling up with tears.

"Yes, a little. But I'll be okay." Kenisha stooped down to hug her daughter. "What a pretty angel you made. Did you have fun in Sunday school today?" She talked like she had come from the dentist, slurring her words and trying uselessly to make her lips move into a smile.

Essie spoke up, concern etched on her face. "Let me fix you some lunch, Kisha, sweetie, then you can take your nap, okay?"

"But I don't want to take a nap." Kisha's automatic response to that word.

"Well, let's eat first. Then I'll read you a nice story and you can just rest if you feel like it. Your mommy needs to rest, too, so she can get better. Will you be a good girl so Mommy can get better?" Essie's voice was both pleading and authoritative.

"Yes, Gramma, I will."

Kenisha put her arm around Kisha's shoulders and steered her toward the breakfast nook. She sat with Kisha as Essie went into the pantry to get the makings for a peanut butter and jelly sandwich. Kenisha drank down the last of her coffee and got up to go upstairs. "Kisha, you be good for Gramma while I go upstairs to take a nap, too, okay?"

"Yes, Mommy. I hope you feel better. Can I kiss it?" She held up her arms to Kenisha.

Kenisha really did smile that time, through the pain. "Kisha, I love you, sweetie. Yes, kiss me on this side." She bent down so that Kisha could kiss her on the right side of her face.

Kisha wrapped her arms around her neck and hugged her, too. "I love you, too, Mommy."

Kenisha's tears started again as she turned and went upstairs. Her daughter's sweet innocence always helped her to cope with whatever she was facing. She knew she had to be strong for Kisha's sake, if for no other reason.

After putting Kisha down for her nap, Essie fixed a grilled cheese sandwich, some tomato soup in a cup, and a glass of water with a straw, and took lunch up on a tray to Kenisha. "Here, baby, you better eat something."

"Thanks, Ma." Kenisha sat up and straightened out the cover over her lap for the tray.

Essie arranged the tray in front of Kenisha and sat on the edge of the bed. The alcohol reeked. She looked over and saw the broken glass by the closet door. Concern lines were deep on her forehead, making her look older. "Did Joe do this to you?"

Kenisha nodded.

Essie jumped up with her fists clenched. "I'm gonna kill him! I'm gonna kill him! That coward, that bastard! I'll kill him!"

Kenisha was surprised at the strength of her anger. "Mom, calm down. Mom!" She reached for Essie's hand and almost tipped over the tray.

Essie looked at her and breathed deeply, snorting as she gathered herself together. After a moment, she calmed down. "I'm sorry, baby, I don't want to upset you anymore, but I can't believe that bastard would do this to you. Look at you." She started to cry. "How could he do this to you? How could he … what did you do?"

Kenisha's face contorted at that question. "I didn't do anything to deserve what he did to me," she replied curtly as she let go of Essie's hand.

Essie was immediately apologetic. She reached out for her daughter's hand and held it tight. "I know that, baby, there's nothing you could do to deserve this. I'm sorry. I just wanted to know what could have happened to bring this on. I know it's not my business. You don't have to tell me if you don't want. I just want to be here for you."

"I know, Mom. I'm glad you're here. It's just that you always take Joe's side when I try to tell you that things aren't going so well. I never like talking to you about me and Joe, because I feel like you want to blame me." Kenisha started to tear up, reached for a Kleenex on the nightstand, and blew her nose. Kenisha had not told her mother before how she felt about her mother's interference in her marriage, but the emotion of the moment made it come out. Kenisha really needed her mother on her side now, and she was afraid that might not happen.

Essie sat down on the edge of the bed and caressed her daughter's hair. "Oh, baby, I'm so sorry" was all she said for several moments, until she looked at Kenisha and spoke quietly. "Baby, I only want what's best for you. I love you with all my heart. If I thought that creep would hurt you, I would never have taken up for him. I just didn't know. I'm so sorry." She put her arm around Kenisha's shoulders and continued to hold her daughter close. After a few moments she said gingerly, "Has he hit you before?"

Kenisha accepted her mother's loving touch. That moment was healing for her. "No, Mom," she said quietly. "He's never hit me before this. But he's been treating me like dirt for a few years now, and I don't really know why."

She paused as she thought about how much she should tell her mother. "Well, I do know something. You know that he's been going out with some woman on the north side for a couple of years now, don't you? Everybody else seems to know." She picked up the cheese sandwich and nibbled on it.

"I heard about it from some busybodies." Essie let go of her daughter and sat up. "But a lot of men cheat on their wives. That's just the way men are. If you just hang in there, he'll come around."

Kenisha riled up again. Essie's "wisdom" just sounded to her like she was taking up for Joe again. Her voice rose angrily. "But that doesn't mean he has to treat me like dirt. I'm sorry, Mom, but you don't know what it's been like. He just doesn't love me anymore, and when he came in last night and started to dress to go back out again, everything just hit the fan." Kenisha knew she couldn't tell her about the fraud that Joe was mixed up in, at least not yet.

"Well, baby, you're right." Essie stood up. "You're absolutely right. You should stand up to him. You don't have to take that from him! You're a beautiful woman and a beautiful person, and he ought to know it and treat you like you deserve to be treated." She put her left hand on her hip and shook her right finger. "And I'll help you make sure he doesn't come back in this house again, at least until the two of you get some counseling. I don't ever intend to let him hit on you again." She started stomping around the bedroom and swinging her arms. "You don't ever have to take that. I won't have you being one of those women whose husbands think they're just punching bags. I didn't raise you like that. I'll shoot the bastard before I let him hit you again."

Essie's anger made Kenisha feel better. She gave Essie a one-sided smile and took another bite of her cheese sandwich. "Thanks, Mom. I tried to get Joe to go to Pastor Keith with me for counseling, but he wouldn't even talk about it. I went to Pastor Keith last week, and he helped me a lot."

"Well, you just don't let Joe back in this house until he's agreed to see Pastor Keith with you. Unless he's willing to try to work it out, you're just setting yourself up to let it happen again. I surely will kill the bastard if he hits you again." Essie flailed her arms again.

The look on Essie's face made Kenisha think Essie really would kill him. "Relax, please, Mom. It won't do me any good to have you in jail. But I'm glad you're on my side. Joe wouldn't know what hit him if you got after him. I can just see it now, you beating him upside the head with a baseball bat." And she started laughing. Essie started laughing, too, and they hugged across the tray and cried together.

Essie sat quietly while Kenisha continued to eat. Essie never realized Kenisha thought she was taking Joe's side against her, but she did know how Kenisha could have come to that conclusion. Essie wanted Kenisha's marriage to go well, and she reasoned that if she couldn't control Joe, she could at least get Kenisha to do what would be necessary to cope with his behavior. To Essie, keeping the marriage intact was the most important thing. She never thought that in the process of directing Kenisha to placate Joe, she was alienating her only child.

After Kenisha finished her food, Essie took the tray. "I'm going to run home while Kisha's still asleep and get me some clothes to wear tomorrow. I'll be right back."

"Oh, Mom, you don't have to stay over. I'll be okay."

"At least for one night, okay, baby? I want to make sure you're okay before I leave you with Kisha. You may need to go to the doctor." Essie had no intention of not staying over.

"No, I think I'm going to be okay. I don't think anything is broken, just bruised up kind of bad."

"Well, let me stay for at least one night, so I'll feel better, okay? I'll help to get Kisha out to school in the morning and pick her up for you tomorrow. Then we can take it from there." She kept asking so that Kenisha would feel like she was making the decision.

"Okay, Mom. I love you." Kenisha always relented. "Will you help me to clean up this mess?" She directed her arm over to the glass and alcohol by the closet.

After helping Kenisha clean up the glass and scrub the carpet, Essie urged her to rest in bed. She then went downstairs, washed up the dishes, and went out the front door, locking it from the inside before she shut it. She quickly drove home, going straight east down Ninety-fifth Street. She was glad that she didn't live that far from her daughter, although the neighborhoods were completely different.

The first thing she did when she walked in the door of her home was to look up Pastor Keith's home number in the church directory. She dialed, and Pastor Keith's wife, Cora, answered. "Hello, Mrs. Summers. I'm Essie Brown, one of the church members. I'm sorry for calling your home, but it's kind of an emergency. May I please speak to Pastor Keith?"

His wife's voice was kind. "Sure, Ms. Brown, just a minute."

"Hello, Ms. Brown. What can I help you with?" Pastor Keith clearly wondered why she was calling him. Even though they knew each other from church, they had only shared pleasantries. Essie couldn't remember having a conversation with him about anything.

"I'm calling about my daughter, Kenisha Cooper. She told me that she's seen you for some counseling about her and her husband, Joe." She stopped for a moment, having second thoughts about revealing her daughter's family crisis to him. But he seemed to be nice, and she was sure he could help Kenisha. Maybe he could even figure out what the problem was with Joe. She went on. "Well, Joe beat her up pretty bad last night, and I was hoping you could stop by the house and talk to her, and maybe even talk to Joe. I don't want him going back to that house. I'm afraid he might hurt her again."

Pastor Keith's concern came through his voice. "I'm so sorry this happened. I'll go by to see Kenisha as soon as I can."

Essie was surprised that he didn't ask any further questions, and at the same time pleased because he cared enough to visit Kenisha right away.

Chapter 15

The Opposers know that fear makes hearts home to secrets. The human creatures keep secrets so well that they often don't even know that's what they are doing. They hide both thoughts and reality, even to themselves. Truth and open honesty, both of which lead to healing, get lost in the secret places of a fearful heart.

Renewal

Pastor Keith rang Kenisha's doorbell at around seven o'clock that Sunday evening. Essie opened it after a moment. "Come in, Pastor Keith."

Kisha ran to hug him. "Hi, Pastor Keith. What are you doing at my house?"

Keith saw Kenisha behind them, moving quickly up the stairs. He spoke loud enough for her to hear. "Hello, Kisha. I'm here to see how your mommy is doing. Is she here?"

"Yes, she's in the kitchen. This way."

Kisha grabbed his hand and started to lead him to the kitchen, when Essie interrupted. "Wait a minute, baby. Mommy went upstairs." She shouted up the stairs, "Kenisha. Pastor Keith's here to see you."

Essie turned to Keith and directed him to the living room. "Hello, Pastor Keith. I'm so happy you came. Won't you come and sit over here? Can I get you something, maybe some tea or coffee?"

"No, but thanks. I'm fine." Pastor Keith sat down on the couch, and Kisha climbed up next to him. Essie sat down in the armchair facing him.

"Thank you for coming. I didn't tell her I called you because I didn't want to give her a chance to say no." Essie spoke in a low, secretive voice.

"I wish you had told me that. I would have called her before coming. But it's okay. I do want to see her. Hopefully I can be of some help." Pastor Keith both chastised her and forgave her at the same time.

Kenisha came down the stairs with a housecoat over her pajamas, wearing a pair of large sunglasses and a Cubs baseball cap. Keith stood to greet her as she came into the living room.

Essie quickly took Kisha's hand. "Kisha, come with me. Want to watch some cartoons on the big Television?"

"Okay, Gramma. Bye, Pastor Keith." She jumped down and headed for the door leading downstairs.

Essie, following Kisha, turned to mouth "thank you" again to Pastor Keith.

Keith turned to Kenisha, still standing. "Kenisha, I'm sorry for surprising you like this. I spoke to your mother earlier today and she told me what happened. I just thought I might be of some help."

Kenisha continued to look down, as if she was trying to hide her face. "Thank you for coming, Pastor Keith. I'm sorry you have to see me like this. Please sit down." She sat down in the chair across from him. "It looks worse than it feels, or maybe that's just because I've been taking pain pills."

"Have you seen a doctor?" He sat down and leaned forward, concerned.

"No, but I don't think anything is broken. I'm just bruised up pretty bad, that's all."

Keith gently scolded her. "Don't try to make light of it, Kenisha. I'm here for you, if you want me to help. Do you want to talk about it?"

She looked up at him. "What I didn't tell you before is that he's been seeing another woman. It's not even behind my back. Everybody knows about it and he's always gone. I hardly ever see him anymore, and when he's here, he doesn't want to talk to me. When I asked to talk to you before, he hadn't come home the night before, and that's not the first time." She pulled a tissue out of the pocket of her housecoat, dabbed her eyes, and sniffed. Her voice became teeny, as if it hurt too much to say the words. "I just didn't know what to do. He came in last night at about ten and started changing clothes to go back out again. I had already been drinking, and it was just too much. I guess I started it, but he shouldn't treat me that way."

"Whatever you may have said or done to him wasn't enough for him to hurt you this way, Kenisha. It's not your fault, and don't you ever think that it is." He spoke authoritatively, clipping his words for emphasis. He knew he should be neutral as her counselor, but she needed to know just how wrong this was. "What happened after he hit you?"

"I don't know what he did. He was gone when I woke up. I haven't seen or heard from him since. Pastor Keith, there was something so evil in him that night, it scared me. I've never seen him like that." She hung her head again.

"He knocked you out?" Keith had a hard time keeping control of his voice.

"Yes," she said, in that small voice with her head down.

"Kenisha, take off your glasses and your cap. I want to see what he's done to you."

She took them off, keeping her head down.

"Look at me." Even to himself he sounded like a father.

She lifted her head. He looked at her intently, sorrowfully. Tears came unexpectedly to his eyes. "Kenisha, you should file a complaint and get a protective order against him. It's not that hard to do. It will keep him away from the house and put the police on alert that he may try to hurt you again."

She looked up at him with pleading eyes. "Pastor Keith, I really don't want to do that. I don't want this to be a public battle. You know how well connected he is. It would just be a big mess, and that would be worse for me. I'm not going to let him hurt me again. All I want to do is find a lawyer and quietly start the divorce proceedings."

Keith backed off. At least she was willing to take some steps to protect herself. "You want me to check to see which attorneys in our church do divorces?"

"No, Pastor Keith, I don't want the church people to know. I'll find someone."

He looked at her intently, again. "Listen, Kenisha. You shouldn't feel ashamed. It's not your fault. Joe is the one who's done wrong, and you shouldn't try to sweep it under the rug or to hide it. You should be angry, not ashamed. There's nothing wrong with righteous indignation over something as sinful as abuse. The more you try to hide it, the more likely it will happen again. So don't go around telling people you ran into a door or fell off a skateboard, do you hear me?" He really did feel as if he needed to be a father for her.

She looked up at him, and he saw in her eyes that she recognized the truth of his words. Her voice was stronger as she said, "Thanks, Pastor Keith. I needed to hear that. I know you're right. It's just so hard to let people know that my life is all messed up."

"Your life may feel like that now, but you'll get through this, Kenisha. And one day you'll be able to look back at it and say, 'Thank you, God, for helping me.' You know that God is with you even in your pain and distress, don't you?" Pastor Keith quickly thought about how often he had to remind people of that. "You know that God doesn't want you to live in a bad situation or to live in fear. Have you been reading the 23rd Psalm like I asked you?"

"Yes, and it has really been helping me to cope. Thank you for suggesting it." She smiled through her swollen lips.

"Well, listen to this." He pulled out a tiny Bible from the inside of his coat pocket and a pair of glasses from the other side, opened the book, and turned the pages. "The Lord is my light and my salvation. Whom shall I fear? The Lord is the strength of my life. Of whom shall I be afraid?" He read through the 27th Psalm, slowly and deliberately, again.

"I want you to read the 27th Psalm each morning and any other time during the day when you feel the need. It will help give you strength, so you'll know that you're connected to God, who is stronger than anything, any power, any evil that might face you, and who loves you with a powerful love." He looked her right in the eyes, as if to drill the strength and love right through her.

"Yes, Pastor Keith. Thank you. I feel better already." She said it as if she meant it.

"Would you like to pray?" he asked as he put the Bible and glasses back in his pocket.

"Oh, yes. Please."

He smiled as they both stood up and held hands.

Chapter 16

The recordings of the faithful are more powerful than most of the children will ever begin to understand. The recorded stories of the Creator's work in the world and the battle between the angelic forces and their Opposers are among the most meaningful tools that the creatures can use to help each other remember who they are. Because of the children's own limited understanding and their desire to exert power over others, the stories are often misused and misunderstood. But for the many faithful, the Creator shines through the written word and speaks truth to their inward spirits. And when the words of truth speak to their souls, the children are empowered to new depths of love, compassion, courage, and faith—the Creator's gifts to all of them.

Strength

That Monday Kenisha slept late, getting up at about 10:00 AM groggy from sleeping pills. "Now I remember why I don't like that stuff," she said to herself as she bumped clumsily downstairs in her pajamas to make some coffee. Essie had already taken Kisha to the nursery school and gone to work. Kenisha had asked Essie to call the rehab office this morning and let them know Kenisha was taking a sick day. She was thankful that her mother was there and that they had finally broken through some of the secrets that had been damaging their relationship.

The quiet house had a pleasant, peaceful feel to it. The morning felt soothing, like an unexpected day off with nothing to do. Maybe it was the effect of the pain pills she was taking. She looked forward to relaxing in her big easy chair in the front room by the bay windows, sipping coffee and reading the paper. She didn't want to think about anything, not yet. If it weren't for her face, this would be a good day.

The phone rang right after the coffeepot started brewing. She saw that it was Joe, calling from his cell phone.

She said to herself, "The Lord is my strength. Of whom should I be afraid?" And she answered the phone. "Hello."

"Hi, Nisha. Look, baby, I'm sorry about what happened Saturday. I don't know what got into me. I saw your car in the drive and thought I better call before I came in. I know you probably don't want me around right now, but I need to get some things. Can I come in?" He sounded sincerely sorry.

"You're here?" She was still trying to get her brain to focus.

"Yeah, I'm right outside."

She walked over to the bay window, peeked out the drawn curtain, and saw him standing by his car at the curb looking at her with the phone to his ear. She walked over quickly to put the chain on the door at the side entry. "Joe, I don't want you in this house."

"Okay, baby. I understand. I didn't mean to hurt you. But I need to get a few things. I'll be gone in just a couple of minutes."

She hesitated, her mind racing now. "Well, give me a few minutes. I'll let you know when you can come in." She went upstairs and pulled out two large suitcases from the closet. Opening his dresser, she put in his underwear, socks, and T-shirts. She went to the closet and pulled out suits, shirts, and shoes, stuffing them in. She cleared off his dresser and threw his shaver, cologne, deodorant, and toothbrush in from the bathroom.

She heard him at the door. He had used his key to open it and was pushing the door against the chain. "The Lord is my strength," she kept saying to herself. She knew he couldn't get in the door through the kitchen patio because they kept a burglar bar on the sliding door when they were not using it, and the door in the basement was bolted from the inside.

"Baby, why do you have the chain on the door? I'm not going to hurt you." He spoke through the opening as he continued to try to push the door open. He couldn't break the chain lock.

She dragged the first suitcase downstairs and then the other one. She carried one of them with two hands and pushed the other with her foot across the hardwood floor to the entry area. "Look, Joe," she said, breathing heavily now. "I'm letting you in to get these suitcases, and that's all. You take these suitcases and then you leave, you hear me?" She tried to sound menacing.

"Yeah, baby, I'll leave." He stopped pushing on the chain.

"You promise me, Joe, or so help me ..."

He didn't respond. He just waited.

She took the chain off and stood ready to close the opened door the moment he walked back out.

He just stood in the doorway for a couple of seconds, looking at her. His hair, usually immaculately pasted down in waves and parted to the side, was disheveled, and he needed to shave. He still had on the same suit from Saturday night, rumpled now, and his tie was gone. Kenisha couldn't help but wonder if his girlfriend threw him out, but she kept silent.

As he walked through the door, he handed her a bunch of roses, the kind sold at the grocery store. "See, I'm really sorry, baby. I don't know what got into me." He leaned forward as if he wanted to hug her.

Her heart trembled as she dodged him. "Take the suitcases and get out of here, Joe." She looked at him with hard and cold eyes.

"Why are you treating me like this? You know I'm sorry. I won't hurt you anymore."

He smelled like stale smoke and alcohol. And for some reason it made her feel pity for him. "Take the suitcases and go, Joe, please." She backed away and picked up her cell phone from the table in the foyer, pointing to the door with it.

"Okay, baby, I'm going. Look, I'm taking the suitcases." He moved them, one at a time, out onto the entry porch.

She stood by the door to shut it when he took the second one out, but he stayed just in the doorway. He turned and said, "Look, you can't keep me away from here. This is my house. I know you're mad at me right now, but this is still my house and Kisha's my little girl. We can get through this, baby." He took a step back in.

She stepped back, fear as well as anger rising. "Look, Joe, I don't want to live like this anymore. I want a divorce."

"A divorce?" A flash of anger crossed his face, but he got it under control. He pushed the door open all the way. "Baby, you don't have to do all that. I'm a changed man. I'm so sorry about what's happened. I want to make it up to you. We just need some time, that's all."

Kenisha moved back into the foyer, still holding onto the cell phone. She thought, *The Lord is the strength of my life.* She was determined to let him know how she felt and not cower away from him like she normally did. "Look, Joe, I don't think we can fix this. This has been going on for too long. I'm not your punching bag. I don't want to live with you when you treat me like dirt. I still don't know what I did to deserve how you treat me."

"It's always about you, isn't it? What about me? I work my ass off to give you everything you want." His face went from pleading to menacing.

She took a couple more steps back. She said to herself, *Of whom shall I be afraid?* "Joe. Leave. Now." Her voice rose as she emphasized each word. "I'm calling the police if you're not out of here. Now." She held up the cell phone.

Her attempt to face up to him only made him angrier. He moved toward her again, menacingly. "You think they could do anything to me? I could kill you before they got here. I could kill you before you even dialed that number." He caught himself and seemed to try to get in control again. His face reverted back to pleading. "Look, baby, I'm sorry. I just don't want us to get a divorce. Besides, God doesn't allow divorces, and you're a good church woman."

She was still trying to be strong, but when he started toward her again, she moved back. Their movements were like a dance, one of intimidation and fear, moving slowly to what seemed an inevitable tragic climax.

"Joe, I've already talked to Pastor Keith about it, and he says God wouldn't want me to live in an abusive situation." In spite of her efforts to not be intimidated, her voice started to crack, and she was now pleading. "Look, I don't want to talk about this now. Just please, get out, now."

Just then her cell phone rang. She answered quickly. "Pastor Keith, I'm so glad you called. Joe's here right now." She looked at Joe with new determination in her eyes. Pastor Keith's calling at this moment gave her the strength she needed. "He was just leaving, weren't you, Joe?"

Joe moved forward, started to say something, then stopped, turned, and stomped out of the house, taking the suitcases with him across the sidewalk to the car.

Kenisha sighed with relief as she shut and locked the door and leaned back against it. "Pastor Keith, you called right on time. Joe came to get his things but didn't want to leave. He still scares me, Pastor Keith. Maybe I should get that protective order after all."

Chapter 17

Lies driven by fear are the Opposers' handiwork, for they serve the Great Liar. Humans have learned to lie so freely that, just as with secrets and greed, they don't even realize that they're lying. And they don't realize that it is fear that drives them to lie. The Great Liar is like the spider, waiting at the edge of the web to devour the flies that become trapped in their own deceit.

Lies and Fear

The first thing Joe did after checking into the Drake Hotel later that Monday morning was to pick up the phone and call Pastor Rowland's office. The pastor's personal secretary, Monique Donahue, answered, quite professionally, as always. "Hello, you've reached Deliverance Church. This is Pastor David Rowland's office, Monique Donahue speaking. May I help you?"

"Hello, Monique. This is Joe Cooper. How are you today?"

"I'm blessed, Mr. Cooper," she said with a friendly, familiar laugh. "How are you?"

"I'm fine, dear. Look, I know Reverend Rowland's not there on Mondays. But I was wondering if you would do me a big favor."

"I'll try. What is it, Mr. Cooper?"

"I need to have just a few minutes of the reverend's time first thing tomorrow morning, if you can squeeze me in. It won't take long."

"Well, you know the Lord must be on your side today, Mr. Cooper. Reverend Rowland just had a meeting that cancelled. He comes in tomorrow at around nine-thirty. I can put you in at nine forty-five if that's okay." She prided herself on her efficiency and loved it when things worked out neatly.

"That's mighty fine, Monique. You are a blessing. I'll see you at nine forty-five, sharp."

"That's Tuesday, June 22, at nine forty-five. See you then," she said efficiently.

He showered, dressed, and hung up the rest of the clothes in the hotel closet. After shaving, he placed a call to Darlene and got her voice mail. "Hi, baby, look, Im sorry for Sunday night. I don't know what got into me. I was just in a bad mood because Kenisha wouldn't let me off the hook. Please let me come over tonight. I'll take you out to dinner, wherever you want to go. Just say yes, please?" After their blowup when they went to dinner Sunday night, Darlene wouldn't let him come back to her place, and he had stayed out all night drinking. He wanted to make up with her because he didn't know how long it was going to take to get Kenisha to come around. He didn't want to spend his money on a hotel room.

He hung up the phone, had his car brought around, and headed to his office on Sixty-fifth and Western Avenue. Darlene called him back right after he got there. She forgave him and told him to come over Monday after work. He smiled to himself. He knew she would forgive him; he always got what he wanted from the women around him.

Tuesday, after Darlene left for work, Joe dressed and left her house to go back downtown to the Drake, get his bags, and check out. After the bellman put his suitcases in the trunk of his car, he headed south to the church for his appointment with Reverend Rowland. The church was in a district that was recovering from worse times. They called it "Bronzeville" now, the heart of the African American community, and new condos were popping up all over the place. The property across the street from the church, which Joe knew Pastor Rowland needed to expand his church's holdings, was worth a lot more than it was ten years ago. Joe liked the fact that his connections could make or break that project.

He arrived about eight minutes late. "Monique, darling. I'm so sorry

I'm late. I hope Pastor Rowland is still available." He looked at Monique with an intentional twinkle in his eye. Joe knew she thought he was handsome, and he willingly used his good looks to gain favors.

"Yes, he actually just got in a few minutes ago himself. Let me tell him you're here." Monique had a soft, husky voice that was easy on the ears. She smiled at Joe as she walked confidently around her desk with a pen and pad in her hand and knocked on Pastor Rowland's door, opened it, and went in, shutting the door behind her. She was wearing a navy blue suit with a tight-fitting long skirt and three-inch heels.

Monique didn't dress like a grandmother or a misfit just because she worked in the church. When she first started working for Pastor Rowland, some of the older women told the pastor that she needed to dress more appropriately. That was when she stopped wearing miniskirts. But the longer skirts were still tight.

She came out a few minutes later. "He's ready for you, Mr. Cooper." She smiled at him sweetly, again.

Pastor Rowland stood and walked over to greet Joe, holding out his hand and smiling. "Hello, my friend. I was surprised when I got the message you wanted to meet with me. How are you? How's business?"

"Hello, Pastor." Joe shook his hand, smiling back. Pastor Rowland's smile was friendly, but Joe always noticed that Pastor Rowland's teeth looked like they were not quite clean, kind of grayish.

Rowland shook Joe's hand and patted him on the right shoulder at the same time as he ushered Joe to one of the ornate Georgian chairs facing his large glass-covered mahogany desk. Rowland was a somewhat tall and thin fifty-six-year-old brown-skinned man with stooped shoulders. His curly hair was gray at the edges and beginning to recede. He had a mustache and a goatee, small eyes, and a large beaklike nose on which his reading glasses perched while he looked over them. Pastor Rowland's claim to fame was a deep, booming voice that he used with great skill while preaching. He was considered a leader in his religious denomination.

In spite of himself, Joe was in awe of this nationally known and well-respected man of the cloth. Around Pastor Rowland's ample office were bookshelves filled with religious tomes and scholarly works. His desk was neat and clean, with one box for papers, a phone, and a few conversation pieces that were placed there to impress visitors with his trips to other parts of the world. A large globe sat in the far right corner. The office impressed on others that Rowland was efficient, effective, well-traveled, well-educated, and well-off.

Rowland had the air of a scholar about him, and that made Joe feel like he needed to prove his own value, which was not in scholastics but in money.

When they were both seated, Joe said, "Business is business. It's all good. I'm here for a couple of reasons."

David Rowland sat back and waited, not happy that Joe was sitting across from him. Joe contributed more than most to the church, but he also knew that what he contributed didn't come close to tithing. Joe served on the trustee board, but he didn't come to church often and never participated in any of the Bible classes or anything else the church did, for that matter. Joe had good connections with the government that he had used to help the church get some grants for an after-school program that was highly popular in the community and helped to give the church a good reputation.

On the trustee board, Joe had a lot to say about how the church handled money, and he was often at odds with some of the more spiritually minded board members who were more concerned with serving the community than saving money. Joe could be useful to the church, but he could also be a pain, and Rowland knew he needed to handle Joe with care. David Rowland didn't want any problems with him, now that they were trying to build a community center across the street next to the park. The community center would serve the additional purpose of providing some much-needed office and classroom space for the church. They needed Joe's money and his connections to buy the last lot needed for the project.

Joe continued, "First, I want you to know that I've got a person who can help us get that building condemned across the street so that we can begin our project. He's in the Building Department. He'll start the process to take eminent domain so the city can tear it down at no cost to the church. I think we have a good case for claiming that the owners have abandoned it." He leaned back and puffed his chest out importantly as he shared this news.

Pastor Rowland smiled. "That's great news, Joe. We knew we could count on you." Pastor Rowland couldn't help but question whether it would be as simple as Joe indicated. Rowland had been around the block a time or two with government agencies, and there was always a catch. But he knew he needed to encourage Joe to do all that he could.

Joe's face turned serious as he sat forward again. "But I'm here mainly for another, personal reason. I really need to understand something that's confusing me." Joe paused and sat forward. He leaned with one hand on the desk and lowered his voice. "It's about something that Pastor Keith Summers said to my wife."

Somehow Rowland knew this was the real reason Joe came to visit him. *It's as if he's got a secret he just can't wait to tell me,* he thought.

"Kenisha and I have been having some marital problems lately, Pastor Rowland. You know what that's like, I'm sure, with all the people you have to deal with. It's nothing unusual." Joe paused as if to let the reasonableness of what he was saying sink in. "Well, Kenisha went to talk with Pastor Keith, and he told her that it would be okay to get a divorce. He even encouraged her. I don't claim to know that much about the Bible, but I thought that divorce was against God's laws. That's what you told us when you married us: 'For better or for worse, until death do us part, under God.' I don't know why he's encouraging her to leave me, but it's upsetting our marriage. I thought you should know about it." Joe sat back, appearing satisfied with the impact of the bomb he had just dropped.

Rowland leaned back on his chair, bouncing his legs a bit nervously as he listened to Joe. He heard the threat quite clearly. He knew Joe well enough to know that not only would Joe pull his support for the project if he didn't get his way, he would also find a way to oppose the project.

Rowland took his time in responding. He had nurtured Keith and his call into the ministry, helped support him through college and seminary, and gave him a job ahead of many others. Keith was a good man, and many members seemed to enjoy his work. He hadn't had any serious complaints about him before. But divorce was one of those areas that Rowland was not willing to be liberal about. Officers of the church had to be, above all, strong family men. This had been a church policy for a long time, and he was not about to start rocking the boat, especially now, when they needed Joe's support to get this building constructed. What was Keith thinking?

Rowland said finally, "I'm shocked, Joe, that Keith would do such a thing. You know that's not this church's official policy. No one can serve an office if they're divorced. I know a lot of churches don't enforce that rule anymore, but it's God's law, not ours to change. I'll have a talk with Keith about it." He looked at him squarely. "Would you like to bring Kenisha with you to talk with me about it?"

"I've already talked to her, and I think we'll be able to work it out. I just wanted you to know what Keith was saying to her. We'll be okay." Joe abruptly stood up, now that his business with Pastor Rowland was done. "Listen, I know you're busy and I've got a couple of appointments myself. Thanks for looking into that for me, Pastor Rowland. I'm going to try to get to church this Sunday."

Pastor Rowland stood with him. "I'm glad you stopped by, Joe. I'll look into that right away." David Rowland's forehead was frowned as he walked Joe out of the office and to the outer door. "You have my assurance that it will not happen again. I'll keep you and Kenisha in prayer. Tell her I said hello."

Chapter 18

The Angels were again disturbed. One of their greatest sorrows is that the children who are called to be religious leaders often don't remember who they are well enough to understand the self-sacrifice and faith needed to hold such special positions. They become blinded to the Creator's reality by the world they see around them and allow the world to define their success. Shortsighted rules they create for purposes of power and control too often become long-standing and unquestioned traditions, with hurtful consequences. If they understood the love that is behind all of the Creator's teachings, they would not allow their own traditions to mislead so many away from the Creator's Plan.

Yet, the beauty of that Plan is that there are always some who see through the blindness and who have the courage driven by love to challenge long-standing but faulty traditions.

Betrayal

Keith was in his office working on a progress report for one of the grants that kept the after-school program operating. He needed to get it done today to get it to the secretary for proofing and copying before he left at noon, to go first for lunch and then to visit a nursing home with some of the deacons. That was the only way the report could be ready to be mailed out by Wednesday. His phone rang, and he glanced at the clock. It was a little after 10:00 AM. Keith was pretty sure he could get the grant done if he didn't have too many disturbances. He started not to answer but thought better of ignoring a call from Pastor Rowland's office.

He picked up. "Hi, Monique."

"Pastor Keith, Reverend Rowland would like to see you, if you can."

"When?" He really didn't want to stop now.

"Right away."

"Oh?" Keith expressed his surprise. Reverend Rowland usually had his days carefully laid out. "What's up?"

"I don't know. I think you better just come on up." There was an urgency in her voice that told Keith this was serious.

Keith's office was on the second floor of the church's three-story building. A reception room, Keith's office, an office that was shared between the church's financial officer and two part-time ministers, and two Sunday school classrooms were on this floor, which also housed the balcony of the sanctuary. As Keith made his way up the stairs to the pastor's office on the third floor, he thought about how tightly all of the staff was squeezed in this building. Keith would be happy for the church to get the community center built across the street. He wanted to move into one of the new offices over there, to be closer to the children. And he had to be honest and admit that he also wanted more room for himself.

Keith arrived at the pastor's reception room no more than five minutes after he hung up the phone, and Monique said, "He's on the phone right now. But I already told him you would be here right away. I don't think he'll be on the phone long. Why don't you have a seat for a couple of minutes? Do you want some tea or coffee?"

"No thank you, Monique. What kind of mood is our fearless leader in?" Keith and Monique shared a bond and often gently joked about Pastor Rowland's moods. They never knew whether they were going to be lectured or whether he would tell them a joke.

"He was in a great mood this morning when he found out that meeting with Ms. Corbine got cancelled. But that all changed after Joe Cooper came over."

Keith was caught off guard. "Oh." He knew something was wrong and wondered at first if Joe could have possibly told David Rowland that he had abused Kenisha. Keith quickly dismissed that thought.

Even if Joe had shared the truth with David, David wouldn't be free to discuss it with Keith. Keith decided that the pastor probably wanted to vent over something that happened relating to building the new community center.

Monique looked at the phone lights. "He's off the phone now. Why don't you knock on the door?"

Keith knocked gently, three times.

"Come on in, Keith." David spoke through the closed door.

When Keith entered, David was standing with his back to the door, looking out the window behind his desk. He said, without turning around, "Have a seat."

"Yes, sir. How are you today, Pastor?"

Pastor Rowland was not one to make small talk when he had something on his mind. He turned around and faced Keith. "Have a seat, please, Keith," he repeated, directing Keith with his right hand to sit in one of the chairs facing his desk.

Keith sat down.

"Keith, I've just heard some disturbing news from Joe Cooper. I'm hoping you'll tell me it's not true. Have you been counseling his wife?"

"I've talked to her a couple of times, yes." Keith braced himself by holding onto both arms of the chair.

"Did you tell her that it's okay for her to divorce?" Rowland sat down and leaned forward with his elbows on the desk, as though he needed to listen carefully to Keith's answer.

Keith looked at David a moment before he spoke, choosing his words carefully. "I wouldn't say it exactly like that. What I told her was the context in which Jesus was speaking when he said it was not lawful for men to divorce women. How much do you know about what's going on with Joe and Kenisha?" Keith knew he had to tread lightly and that he couldn't talk to David about anything that Kenisha had revealed to him in counseling.

"I know that he's upset enough to withdraw his support from the building project." He paused to let that sink in. "Look, Keith, I know that you and I don't agree on everything. We all went to school. We know what they teach in seminary is not always best for the people's understanding. This church has stood against divorce for as long as it has been in existence, and I'm not about to change that now, especially with somebody like Joe Cooper, who we need in order to get this project done." David's stress showed only in the intensity of his words, as he spoke not so loud that those in the outer office could hear but still, quite forcefully.

David's references to the building project only served to irritate Keith, and he sat forward to share his honest and straightforward opinion. He looked David straight in the eyes. "David, I'm truly sorry that Joe is upset. My intention was to help Kenisha understand the biblical record on divorce more deeply. I did not intend to encourage her to get a divorce. That was her decision. But I must say that we both know what Jesus was trying to get across to those men when he spoke against divorce. The most important thing for Jesus, and for me, is that people know that they are not to cause anyone else to suffer for their own selfish reasons. And women like Kenisha need to know that they do not have to suffer at the hand of others just to abide by a rule that clearly was not intended for them." Keith didn't intend to sound quite so combative, but the words just seemed to come out that way.

"Keith, how long have you been with me now?" David's voice was calm now, but as he leaned back and seemed to relax, Keith felt the imminent threat.

"I've been working for you for six years since I graduated seminary. Counting seminary, add three more. And I've been a member here with my family just about all of my life." Keith drummed the desktop with the fingers of his right hand.

"I've watched you grow, Keith, and you're an excellent addition to our staff. But I am the pastor here. You've known from the beginning what we teach on divorce. I can't have you undermining me. I'm afraid you've left me with no other options. Keith, you're going to have to find another place for your ministry. I'll give you thirty days' pay, but you'll have to clear out your office by the end of the week."

Keith's response was to look at David with his mouth open and his eyes wide. He didn't know what to say. He felt as though a ton of bricks had just been dumped on him. "But … how can you do this to me? You know I have a family. What will I tell Cora?" He wanted to say more, but words would not come.

David looked at him steadily over his glasses, his eyes held no signs of remorse. "I'm sorry, Keith, but my decision is final. I'll give you a good recommendation if you need it."

Keith slowly rose from his seat, turned, and walked out the door and out of the office, not saying anything to Monique. He returned to his office and sat at his desk, trying to comprehend what just happened. He'd never been fired from any job before. He'd never been without a job his whole adult life. How he would support his family was his greatest worry. Cora was an elementary school teacher, but with three children, they couldn't make ends meet on her salary alone, and she had been talking about going back to school after they got his seminary debt paid off next year.

He felt like he was set adrift in a large sea without a paddle, nothing to hold onto and with no place to go. As that thought came to him, so did the words to one of his favorite hymns. He heard the choir singing in his head: "Without Him I could do nothing. Without Him I would fail. Without Him my life would be rugged, like a ship without a sail." Remembering that song helped him to remember God, who had always helped him get through difficult times. He knelt down on his knees, right in front of his desk, and prayed sincerely for God's guidance and God's help, for strength, for wisdom, and for peace. He quietly prayed for a long time, until there were no more words. Then he stayed on his knees for some time more, allowing his spirit to be fed by God's spirit. When he got up from that prayer, he felt the peace that always came to him when he felt God's presence. He also stopped worrying, felt stronger, and was able to start thinking about what he would do next.

There were a couple of things he knew he had to do before going home to talk with Cora. He dialed the new minister, Angela Livingston, on the intercom and had her come to his office to give to her the grant report he was working on. He told her what to look for in finishing the review and to get it back to the director of the after-school program by the end of the day and to make sure it got mailed out by Wednesday. He didn't want his departure to take away from the children who they served. He then looked up AAA Trucking in the yellow pages, gathered his briefcase, and left, telling Vanessa that he'd be back in the morning.

Chapter 19

The angelic hosts sang, rejoicing that there are so many beautiful children who are able to remain faithful in their dedication to the Creator's purposes. When the children remember, they become open to what can be done through them. Even with limited understanding, those who open their hearts to the work of the Creator can be powerful allies against the Opposers. And they don't know how much power they can wield until they are forced to tap into the spirit that is in each of their souls—that spirit is who they truly are, and through it they connect to and are empowered by the higher spirits. They sang down songs of power and strength to feed Keith's soul.

New Life

Keith was ushered into Joe's office without delay after he was announced that Tuesday afternoon. Joe's office was nondescript, like an office at an auto mechanic's shop. AAA Trucking Company's headquarters was a huge brick, one-story, square, squalid-looking building that housed the general office, a reception room, Joe's office, and a large area where trucks were brought in for repairs. A few drivers and mechanics were gathered in a small kitchen/employees' room, smoking and playing cards in the front of the building next to the reception area. Outside, the company's territory took up a half block. A gravel parking lot, now mostly dirt, was home to idle trucks surrounded by a chain-link fence topped with barbed wire.

Joe's office was in the back of the building. The desk, cabinet, and file cabinets were old and metal. Mounted on the wall across from the desk was a forty-inch flat-screen Television, the only modern piece of equipment in the office. Joe's desk was scattered with invoices and copies of receipts, old newspapers, and used paper plates. An old brown leather couch sat on the right of the room, and a dirty window with dusty blinds half-open was on the left.

Joe had his feet up on the desk and a cigarette dangling out of his mouth with an intentional frown as he looked at Keith standing there in front of him. He spoke with disdain. "Why are you here?"

Keith shut the door behind him. "I'm here first of all because I've just been fired by Pastor Rowland."

Joe took his feet off the desk and put the cigarette out in a dirty ashtray. "Well, I can't do anything about that, can I? It serves you right, Keith, for meddling in my marriage." He glared at Keith.

"I'm not here because I want you to help me, Joe. I'm here to tell you to stay away from Kenisha. I know what you did to her, and I'll bring the police and everybody else I can down on you if you go near her again." Keith's voice was low but strong and intimidating.

Joe stood up, slammed his fist on the desk, and roared, "Who the hell do you think you are? You have no right to tell me what I can and cannot do with my wife or anybody else. She's mine, and I'll do damn well what I please, and you and nobody else can stop me!"

"You don't have a right to abuse her, Joe. And I won't let you!" Keith shouted back, completely in control of himself and not intimidated by Joe's belligerence.

Joe reached in his drawer and pulled out a gun, a Beretta 92 automatic pistol. "Don't you know I'll kill you, motherfucker? Now get out of here, before I really lose my temper." He pointed the gun first at Keith and then at the door.

Keith was surprised to find that he was not afraid. "Joe, I know you better than this." His voice was now intentionally calm. He looked straight into Joe's eyes, not at the gun. "What's happened to you? You didn't used to be like this."

Joe glared straight back at Keith. "What's happened to me? Nothing that I can't fix by putting you out of my office." Joe came around the desk. "I don't need you to come in here trying to tell me what to do. I don't need you messing in my life. And I especially don't want you talking to my wife!" He grabbed Keith by the jacket, pointing the gun at him again, more and more agitated. "What is it, Pastor?" he sneered. "You want some of Kenisha? Is that it? You're trying to get in her pants by making me look bad? You trying to get her to divorce me so you can have her? Is that it? Huh? You preachers are all alike. Acting all holy, when you're just like everybody else. No, worse, because you're all just a bunch of phonies—lying, cheating, stealing, and womanizing. Is that it, Keith? You want my woman? Huh?"

Keith saw pure evil in Joe's eyes. He was surprised to hear his own voice, deep and resonant, as if it was coming from somewhere else. "Get thee behind me, Satan!" His voice got louder. "In the name of Jesus, I cast you out!"

It wasn't what Joe expected and caught him off guard. Still holding the gun to Keith's head, he looked at him, puzzled.

Keith felt strength go through him. He put his left hand on Joe's head and said it again. "In the name of Jesus, get thee out. In the name of the Father, the Son, and the Holy Spirit, demon, I cast you out!" Then, he held his right hand straight up, and as words that he didn't understand came out of him, he felt a surge of power go through his hand to Joe. They stood locked like that for at least a couple of minutes, Keith mumbling strange incomprehensible words with his hand on Joe's head, and Joe standing there in awe with the gun dangling from his hand, until Joe fell limply to his knees and dropped the gun on the floor.

Joe let out a loud sob. "Oh my God. Jesus. Oh God." He sobbed loudly.

Keith got down on his knees, held Joe's hands, and began praying. "Oh God, thank you for saving this poor lost soul. Thank you, God, for bringing Joe back to us. We praise you, God, for your power. We praise you for your grace. We praise you for your ever-loving presence. Oh, Lord, please stay with Joe. Please keep him safe in your care. Help him to know that you are more powerful than all the evil that wants to take him from you. Thank you, Lord. Thank you for giving him his life back."

Keith took the gun from Joe and helped him to his feet and over to the couch. He sat there until Joe was spent from crying.

Joe leaned forward with his elbows on his legs and his head in his hands. "I don't know, Pastor Keith. I don't know. What have I done?" He looked at Keith as if Keith held the answers. "What have I done? Oh, God, I'm so sorry." Joe's repentance was genuine. "I don't know what got into me."

Keith knew Joe's words were from deep within. "It's okay, Joe. It's okay now. You need to confess your sins before Christ, and he will forgive you."

"But you don't know, Pastor Keith. You don't know what I've done. I'm a thief and a liar, and I beat my wife."

"There's nothing you can do that God can't forgive you for, Joe. Absolutely nothing. As long as you truly repent in your heart. And as long as you do everything you can to make it right again. You remember the thief who was on that cross with Jesus? All he did was believe that Jesus was the Christ and asked to be in heaven with him. That's all you have to do. Do you believe that Jesus is the Christ?"

"Yes." Joe sobbed again.

"Do you repent for all of your sins?"

"Yes, I really do."

"Then your soul is saved, Joe. The devil no longer has a hold on you. Jesus has given you victory over sin and death." They prayed again, praising God again for saving Joe's soul.

After praying, Keith stood and looked down at Joe. "Joe, you have to make things right, now. That's the way to prove that you've truly changed in your heart. That's the way to prove to Jesus that you want to please him."

Joe looked up at Keith with pleading eyes. "You don't know, Pastor Keith. I've done so much. I've been running this business on a sham for the last three years. I could go to prison for what I've been doing; there's no way out. It's the mob, Pastor Keith. They'll kill me if I try to stop it now."

Keith felt Joe's dilemma deeply. "I know it may seem impossible, Joe. But you have to remember that nothing is impossible for God. God is bigger and stronger than even the mob."

Joe stood to face Keith directly. "I don't know what to do, Pastor Keith. But I'm willing to try. I feel like a different person. I don't know, I haven't felt like this in a long time—like I'm free. Like chains have been broken from around my heart. Oh, I need to talk to Kenisha. She probably hates me, but I really want to see her to tell her I'm sorry for what I've done to her."

"Yes, you need to atone for what you've done to her. She's a good woman, Joe." Keith put his arm around Joe's shoulder.

"You're right. I really don't deserve her. It was just that, after the baby was born, I felt like there was so much pressure on me to provide for them. And I was under pressure from the mob, just like most of the other truckers. It seemed to be the right solution at the time, but I knew it was wrong and that I couldn't keep on doing it, and somehow in my head I blamed it all on Kenisha. I felt that she didn't really love me and that all my problems were her fault." His eyes continued to plead for forgiveness. "I could have killed her, Pastor Keith." He sobbed loudly.

"Yeah, you hurt her pretty bad. But she's a good woman. And I'm sure if she knows that you've truly got God in your heart now, you can make it up to her. It may take some time, but time heals all wounds. You'll also be able to work out your other problems if you're truthful, Joe. You'll have to pay for what you've done wrong, but that's the only way to a better future for you and your family." Keith put a hand on Joe's shoulder. "I'll go with you, if you want, to talk to Kenisha. That would be a good place to start."

"Pastor Keith, that would mean a lot to me. Listen, I'm sorry about your job, too. I'm going to talk to Pastor Rowland."

"Don't you worry about me and Pastor Rowland. I can take care of that. I'll call Kenisha. If she says it's okay, can you meet me over at the house tomorrow evening, say around seven?"

"Yes. Let me know what she says."

"I don't expect her to be very forgiving, yet. She's still in a lot of pain, both mental and physical. But we'll tell her what has happened here, at the very least, and take it from there one step at a time." Keith shook Joe's hand, gave him another huge hug, and went home to talk to his wife, Cora, about this amazing day.

Chapter 20

The Opposers roiled in angry dark billows. They had had the weak one in their grips and thought he would be the foiler. They hadn't expected Keith to be used so powerfully by their enemies. Joe was no good to them now. They could direct their energy on the one called Kenisha, but they know that she is strong. The only thing that rivaled the power of love-driven courage against them was love-driven forgiveness.

They normally would work on the pain in her heart to induce an angry self-righteous desire for retribution. But they decided to let things run their course. If she were strong enough to forgive, that would have the effect of keeping her in the marriage, thereby working against the enemy's Plan for her and Michael. They squealed in eerie laughter at the thought that they would foil the enemies' plans using Kenisha's willingness to forgive.

New Hope

When Kenisha answered the door, Keith was standing in front of Joe, as if protecting or hiding him. She wasn't sure which. Essie, who had convinced Kenisha to let her spend the week, took Kisha downstairs to watch cartoons before the men came in. Kenisha did not smile when she greeted them. She wore blue jeans and a blue loose-fitting knit top. Her black-and-blue face was no longer swollen out of shape, and her eye was open now. She led both men into the living room without a word. As they sat down, she stood with her arms crossed, foot tapping.

"I certainly was surprised you wanted to bring Joe over here, Pastor Keith. And he surely would not be here if it were not for you." Her lips were tight as she spoke, not intending to hide her anger.

Keith opened in a soothing voice. "Kenisha, thank you for letting us come. I understand how this must be confusing to you. After I spoke with you yesterday morning, I didn't want Joe anywhere near you. I went over to his office to tell him that, too. But something happened when we talked. Joe had a spiritual experience when I was with him. It was an amazing intervention by God, Kenisha." Keith sat forward and looked directly at Kenisha, his eyes shining with sincere excitement. "I know it might sound strange, but it really happened—the spirit poured out on Joe and released him from Satan's grip. I truly believe Joe is a changed man, or else you know I would not have brought him here."

Kenisha looked at him and then at Joe, who had been nodding in affirmation as Keith spoke. She unfolded her arms and put her hands on her hips, eyes wide. "Whew. I didn't see that coming. You have to forgive me, Pastor Keith, but this is hard to believe." She paused as she sat down. "I don't know what to say." She looked at the two of them, waiting to hear what more they had to say.

Joe spoke up, moving forward on his chair and looking directly at Kenisha with pleading eyes. "Kenisha, all I can say is that I am really sorry for hurting you. This time I really mean it. I don't have any real excuses for all that I did to you. But something really did happen when Pastor Keith laid his hands on me. I felt a power or something coming into my life and making my heart feel full of pain and guilt and sorrow for how I've been living. I turned my life over to Christ, and now I feel like a new man. I know it's hard for you to believe, but it's true. The first thing I wanted to do was to come over and apologize to you."

Kenisha could only snort out a "hmmph" as she looked at him. He really did look different, more like the Joe she married. But not even that Joe. She wrestled in her mind for a description and settled on "humble." She had never seen him look humble before.

Pastor Keith spoke up. "Kenisha, I didn't bring Joe here to get you to take him back. I brought him because I wanted you to hear about what happened."

Before he could say more, Joe cut in. "Kenisha, honey, I'm not asking you to take me back, either. At least not yet. I really do want to make things right again. You'll see. I just wanted to let you know how sorry I am for what I did. I'll make it up to you, surely I will."

Kenisha replayed the scene of her being beaten in her mind, and she stiffened. Sitting straight up in the chair and recrossing her arms, she responded with anger still in her voice. "I know that I'm supposed to forgive you, Joe, but it's just too hard right now. I'm still in pain! I would like to believe that what you say is true. I've learned to trust Pastor Keith. But I honestly can't say that I forgive you right now."

"That's okay, Kenisha. I understand. I just want you to know I'm sorry." Joe seemed to be truly sorry.

Is it just an act? she thought, and she took her time responding. Finally, she said, "Joe, Pastor Keith, thank you for coming by. I will think about what you've said, and I will pray about it and try to learn to forgive Joe in my heart. That's all I can promise right now." The thought of Joe coming back brought back that old feeling of being trapped, and it was unsettling.

"That's all we're asking, Kenisha. That's all we have a right to ask of you." Pastor Keith stood up to leave.

"Before you go, though, I need to speak to Joe about something." She rose and put her hand up as if to stop Keith. "But you stay right here, Pastor Keith." Keith stood still.

Kenisha turned to face Joe, who had started to rise but sat back down. She again took her time, as though she were searching for words. The words finally spurted out, as if they broke loose from being dammed in too long. "Joe, I have information from a lawyer who I met through my job about the truck company fraud investigation that was in the newspaper the other day. He told me they believe that you're involved in it. Is it true?" She decided to bring it up now, with Keith here. It would be one way to test Joe's change of heart.

Keith sat back down. Joe leaned back on the seat, mouth working to try to find the words that were lost in the surprise. He looked at her with an open face, seemingly resigned to tell the truth. He sighed before he spoke. "Yes. It's true. I told Pastor Keith when we talked this afternoon that I had got caught up in something illegal, and I didn't know the way out. It's real messed up right now, baby. I don't know what to do, but I'm going to pray about it and try to figure it out. I may have to do some time." He choked up.

She was surprised that he answered her so honestly. She felt her heart soften some more. "Look, Joe. This attorney that I know can help. He wanted me to tell you that if you came in to help them while they are still gathering information, they might be able to work out a deal for you. I wanted to tell you that before, but I'm not even supposed to know this information, and you, you …" She choked up, too.

"That's all right, baby. I know what I did. God, what a fool I've been." Joe's tears rolled freely down his face. "If you want me to, I'll talk to your lawyer friend. I'll do anything to win back your trust. I love you, Kenisha. You and Kisha are all I have now."

When they left, Kenisha stood at the door for a long time, without closing it behind them, just looking out into the warm summer evening, marveling at what they told her. She thought it would be good to have her old Joe back, or better yet, a new improved Joe. But the thought also left her feeling trapped, and she didn't know why. She wanted to forgive him, but it would take a lot to get her to trust him again. She finally closed the door. She called down to Essie to bring Kisha upstairs to get ready for bed. Kenisha gave Kisha her bath, put her to bed, and then she sat down in the kitchen with Essie and, over a cup of tea, told her mother everything. They cried together and then prayed together for the first time in many years.

Chapter 21

The angelic hosts sang songs of peace and joy. How could they not be filled with joy now that the child, Joe, who was lost, is now back safely in the Creator's arms? And they would rather lose this part of the Plan than to have Kenisha hold onto her anger and damage her soul. That would be much worse. They wanted Kenisha to deepen her compassion and find the healing power of forgiveness in her heart. If she can't do that, she would no longer be able to carry out her part in God's Plan, even if she did divorce Joe and marry Michael.

And the Angels know that even when it seems impossible, especially when it seems impossible, Love will find a way. They knew that the Creator had something in the works that none of them could see.

Atonement

Kenisha decided to go to work on Wednesday. Her face looked a lot worse than she felt. Her spirit had been lifted by the conversation with Pastor Keith and Joe, but all of this was too complicated to relate to anybody. The sunglasses she wore seemed to bring more attention to her face. Germaine Kennedy, the nurse who worked on the sixth floor, asked her what kind of door ran into her. She asked him if that was supposed to be funny, and he said he just wanted to provide a little levity to make her feel better. Some people were quite rude in their effort to be caring! And some of them were just plain nosy. She heard

Pastor Keith's voice telling her not to say she had run into a door, but she still couldn't tell people that her husband beat her up. The people who she knew well respected her wishes not to talk about it. And she just told the ones who kept asking to mind their own business.

Kenisha waited until lunchtime when no one else was in the office, got Michael's cell phone number from his file, and dialed.

"Michael, this is Kenisha. Can I speak to you?"

"Yes, Kenisha. I'm on my way to pick up a sandwich for lunch. Tell me what's going on."

"Joe wants to come in. I think he should talk to you first, before going to the other attorney. Is that possible?"

Michael hesitated and then said, "Okay. Meet me at the Riverwalk, in front of the Vietnam Memorial off State Street, tomorrow, at one o'clock."

Against his common sense, Michael had decided that it was important for him to protect Kenisha from her husband's criminal actions. He figured he owed it to her for helping him through his rehabilitation. Besides, he said to himself, *I just think she's a good person. I like her.* Once his mind was made up, he was able to relax with his decision, but he knew that he still had to be careful.

On Thursday, he told his secretary he had a lunch date and might be late getting back. He took a cab over to Wacker Drive and State Street and headed down the ornate stairway just off State Street to Chicago's Riverwalk. It was a bright, clear sunny June 24, and the Riverwalk was packed with lunchtime workers and sightseers. He sat on a wrought-iron bench in front of the Vietnam Memorial, watching sightseeing boats loaded with tourists, water taxis, and jet skis navigate the murky river water. He marveled at the beauty of the old Tribune Tower across the river to his right, which was overwhelmed by the construction of the Trump Towers directly in front of him. He couldn't help but wonder whether such a big building was going to dwarf the rest of the buildings. To his left were the now historic twin Marina Towers with yachts docked below them as if in a parking lot. Even though he had lived in Chicago all his life, he was still amazed by the beauty of Chicago's skyline.

He saw Kenisha first, about thirty yards away, and then he spotted

Joe next to her. He stood up so that they could see him and leaned over the railing looking out over the river. She came over to stand at his right side, with Joe on her right side. He never looked at her directly. Kenisha seemed to understand how important it was to Michael that they not be seen talking together. She turned away from Michael, faced Joe, and told Joe to talk to Michael.

Joe turned toward her and began talking as Michael continued to look out over the railing. "Look, I hear they think that I'm in on that truck scheme. I've got some information you can use. I can give you some information."

Michael turned away from them, looked around as if he were waiting for someone, and then turned back to the rail. "We need you to name names. Can you do that?"

Joe answered without hesitating. "Yes." His voice was strong and clear, as if he was committed no matter what the outcome was. "I know the connections. What can you do for me?"

"I don't know what they'll do. It's not my case. But I know that if you can connect them to somebody on top, they'll be willing to deal. I can't promise you anything, but if you're willing to wear a wire, you have negotiating power. Are you up to it?"

"Yes."

"Good. I'll leave the card of a good defense attorney on the bench. Call her first, and then have her make arrangements to meet with Julia Dressen. She's the U.S. Attorney on this case." Michael sat down on the bench behind him, took the card out and his phone at the same time, pretended to make a call, and then got up, leaving the card behind him. He then walked unhurriedly over to Michigan Avenue and went up the stairs to find a place to eat lunch before heading back to the office.

Before leaving the Riverwalk, Joe told Kenisha he was going to look for an apartment, and that he'd like to see Kisha on Sunday if possible. She said she'd think about it. He waited until she got a cab back to the hospital, then he walked the six blocks or so over to the Palmer House, where he had been staying since Tuesday. He had several calls to make.

Roslyn Freedman—of Freedman, Gording, and Townsend—was willing to meet with Joe that evening. He made it a point to arrive on time. The law office was a tastefully remodeled large three-story Victorian on West Schiller Street in Old Town. Roslyn was one of the founders of this small law firm, now well established after ten years. She was the criminal defense attorney of the group and specialized in federal cases. She knew all of the attorneys in the U.S. Attorney's Office well.

Roslyn ushered him into her tastefully decorated but cluttered office. "How did you get my name?"

"A friend of my wife's told her to have me call you." Joe felt this woman was the epitome of a female trial attorney. She had platinum blonde, medium-length, somewhat frizzy hair, and she wore a navy blue pin-striped suit with a low v-cut red knit top. She wore spiked heels and brightly painted nails. Joe figured she was around forty, trying to look twenty-five. She spoke to him as if she had known him all her life, with a raspy, alto voice, and looked directly into his eyes. He sensed that there was no fear in her.

"What's your wife's friend's name?"

"I don't remember. Somebody she works with."

"Well, you've come to the right place." She stopped asking him about that. She went on to tell him all about herself and her work and to describe what her fees would be and how they would proceed if they both decided she would represent him.

After she finished getting the details ironed out, she asked him what she could do for him.

He sat forward on the edge of the chair and looked directly at her. He decided to start with a confession. "I can tell you now, Ms. Freedman, I want to plead guilty. I know what I've done, and I want to see if I can win some time by giving the Feds information."

One painted eyebrow arched up. "That's interesting. Tell me more."

Joe proceeded to talk about how he became involved with organized crime to front for their trucking business, how he was told he needed to grease the wheels of government to get more business, and who was involved. She pumped details out of him until she was satisfied. "I'll call the U.S. Attorney's office tomorrow morning. If I'm not mistaken, they'll be anxious to hear what you have to tell them. Can you be available tomorrow?"

Joe answered without hesitation. "Yes."

Chapter 22

The hurtful power of secrets is destroyed by honesty. Truth brings healing when trust has been broken. The Opposers coil back in pain as Joe unravels the web that he has weaved with his greed and lies. But they are not finished with him yet.

Truth

On Friday, first thing in the morning, Julia Dressen's secretary buzzed her. Julia had told her not to interrupt her with calls that morning. She had a lot to do. The *Sun-Times* article last Saturday had been a surprise to her office. They weren't ready to bring the indictments because they had not yet been able to find out how high this thing went. They were leaning hard on the people they knew but getting nowhere. Frank Divine was increasingly impatient now, pushing her to get the FBI to finish the investigation so that she could file and make the case public. He was under pressure from the head office. She was under such pressure that she was almost sorry she had this case.

"Why are you buzzing me?" Julia didn't try to keep her irritation in check.

Her secretary was apologetic. "I'm sorry, Julia, but it's Roslyn Freedman. She said you would be very upset if you didn't take this call.

She relented, now curious. She knew Roslyn, didn't like her, but respected how well she represented her clients. "Okay, I'll take it." Her secretary put the call through.

"This is Julia Dressen."

Roslyn rasped, "I'm going to make your day, sweetheart."

"What is it, Roslyn?" Julia didn't feel like playing games with her this morning.

"I've got a client who wants to work a deal on the truck scandal. He can name names."

"Oh?" Julia was intrigued. She wanted to make sure she bagged some big fish on this one, but she didn't trust Roslyn as far as she could throw her. Julia had her eyes set on the mayor's office, not just the Transportation Department. She was sure this was bigger than Jon Cunningham, the Transportation Department employee who handled the contracts with the trucking companies and who took the bribe money from Mark Garoway, who was the mob connection. If Roslyn had someone who could name the higher-ups, it might be the break she needed.

"Yeah, for real. Do you want to talk to him?"

Julia felt like a hungry fish in front of whom Roslyn was dangling a big, fat juicy worm. "Why don't you bring him in. No promises, you know that. Who is it?" Julia didn't expect her to tell her.

"You'll find out. How about one o'clock this afternoon?"

"Fine."

Julia stood when the secretary led Roslyn and Joe into the conference room. Around a long mahogany table with her were a law clerk, a transcriber, and two FBI agents, John Turkel and Jorge Martinez. She watched Joe begin to sweat in the cool room. Julia introduced everyone to Rosyln and Joe and told them that this session would be recorded.

"As I told Julia over the phone, my client, Joe Cooper, has important information concerning who is involved in your trucking case." Roslyn smiled as she directed her eyes around the table, pausing for dramatic effect. "He's willing to enter a guilty plea, but we need something in return." She turned to Julia.

Julia was impatient. "What do you want, Roslyn?" She thrummed her fingers on the table.

"Probation only. No time, no penalties."

"You know that I can't offer you anything until I have some idea of what your client has to say and how trustworthy is his testimony." Julia intentionally ignored Joe as she dealt with first things first.

"My client," Roslyn turned to Joe, then back to those at the table, "has intimate knowledge about who's involved above the transportation department, as well as the organized crime connection." She smiled again. "I won't let him reveal anything more unless I know that you're willing to deal."

Julia said. "We're open to negotiate for his testimony. I need to hear more before I can promise you probation only."

Roslyn turned to Joe again and nodded to him to begin talking.

Joe told his story, starting with his friendship with a person who connected him to a truck company when he was looking for a job as a business manager after graduating from the University of Illinois with an MBA. He took the job, and after one year, the owners offered to "sell" him the business so that they could take advantage of the minority set-aside provision to get more city work. He became the owner according to the corporate documents filed with the state, but they continued to run the business and take the profits. He was paid well for cooperating and for keeping his mouth shut. They implied they would turn over the business to him one day. He agreed to do it, thinking it wouldn't really be harmful.

A few years ago the business changed hands, but he was still the owner of record. He was told by the new purchasers that he would have to help them to "oil the wheels" to get more business if he was to keep his job. That's when he came to understand that they were being tagged by organized crime. Every month or so, he took a plain envelope with five thousand dollars cash out of the company's funds and gave one-half to a shady character who he only knew as "Moe" and the other half to an official in the transportation department, Jon Cunningham. They received priority in trucking contracts, many of which were shams, so their trucks sat idle while they were paid nicely by the city.

When he finished, Julia intentionally looked bored. "We already know about Cunningham. So far, you've given me nothing."

Joe wiped the sweat off his forehead with a handkerchief. "The person who introduced me to AAA is now the deputy mayor, Clarence Harding. I didn't know he was in on it at first, and I set up a luncheon meeting with him so I could tell him about Cunningham. But Harding already knew. He told me to keep quiet if I wanted to keep the money flowing."

"That's it?" Julia asked, looking at Joe again as though his testimony wasn't of any value.

Roslyn took over. "That ought to be enough. Harding is aware of the bribes and no doubt on the take. We don't know if it goes up any higher. This is trustworthy information that takes the case up to the deputy mayor's office. What more could you ask for?"

Julia turned to her and spoke almost derisively. "I could ask for more proof. We need something to back up his testimony or it's not worth a pile of beans." She turned to Joe. "I need you to get Harding to admit his knowledge. Better yet, get him to admit he's on the take. You'll have to wear a wire, or it's no deal."

Roslyn spoke up again. "The deal is, for wearing a wire, no time in prison. You will charge him with fraudulent violation of the minority hiring statute, and that's all. One year probation for first-time offender, no time served." She tapped her painted nails on the table.

Julia couldn't just go along with everything Roslyn proffered. She leaned forward, as if to physically push Roslyn back. "Two years probation, and a $20,000 penalty."

Roslyn countered, "Two years probation, no penalty."

Julia frowned, "A $10,000 penalty. Bottom line."

Roslyn looked at Joe, who nodded. "Deal."

Julia looked at the agents, who shrugged. "Deal."

Julia allowed herself a tight-lipped smile. "We need the information as soon as possible or it's no-go. I can't keep delaying this case. You'll need to get the information this weekend." Julia looked at the agents. "When can you wire him up?"

Agent Turkel spoke up. "We can hook him up anytime he's ready." He turned to Joe. "When you make the contact, let us know. We'll wire you up and come along for the ride." He gave Joe his card.

As Julia led Roslyn and Joe out of the office, she thought Roslyn's grin looked a little too wicked. Julia decided it was because this was such easy money for Roslyn.

After leaving the attorney, Joe returned to his room at the Palmer House hotel at about 3:30 PM. He was both nervous and excited. He felt as if he was on the right track for the first time in a long time, even though he knew this predicament could put him in jeopardy. He was focused, though. He wanted nothing more than to prove to Kenisha that he really did want to get his life straight. Both the thought of a happy family life with her and Kisha and the memory of his transformation with Pastor Keith fueled his will to go through with it.

Joe used his cell phone to call Clarence Harding. He and Clarence had been drinking buddies more than business partners, so Joe thought he'd invite him out for some fun. His call to Clarence's office was put through to Clarence's cell phone.

When Clarence answered, Joe tried to sound normal. "Hey, buddy, it's Joe Cooper. I thought you might have some time for a couple of rounds tomorrow. It's going to be a nice day for some golf."

Clarence seemed happy to hear from him. "Wish I could, Joe. But Saturday's already taken. How you doing, man? Long time no hear."

"I'm doing okay. But I really need to see you for a few minutes, anyway. You got some time tomorrow? It's important." Joe knew Clarence would not commit to a Saturday meeting unless he thought it was either going to be fun or important for Clarence.

"What's up?" Clarence responded with a serious, business voice.

"I can't talk to you about it over the phone, but you need to hear this. It's a message from our friend Moe." Joe thought the reference to the mob connection would reel Clarence in.

"Look, Joe. It'll have to wait until Monday. I've promised to take the wife and kids to the Taste tomorrow afternoon, and I have an engagement in the morning."

"Look, you really need to know this before Monday. What if I meet you at the Taste just for a few minutes?" Joe's voice communicated a real sense of urgency, which was how he felt.

Clarence relented. "Okay. Meet me on the south side of Buckingham Fountain at 1:00 PM. I'll sneak away from the family for a few minutes."

"Great. You won't be sorry."

After Joe hung up, he started thinking what lie he could tell to get Clarence to talk. He then pulled out Agent Turkel's card and called him. "Listen, it's set for 1:00 PM tomorrow, at the Taste, near Buckingham Fountain."

"Good job. Come by our office, 2111 West Roosevelt, at noon and we'll hook you up. We'll be in the vicinity in case you may need us, as well. I'll let the attorney know."

Julia did not appreciate the four o'clock staff meeting on Fridays. It made more sense to her to meet on any weekday other than Friday, when everyone wanted to wind down and go home. Sometimes the meetings went on for more than two hours, which made her impatient and irritable. If she didn't catch the 6:23 Metra to Elmhurst, the next one wasn't until 7:03, and she wouldn't get home until after 8:00. That irritated her husband. He liked for them to have dinner as a family, and on Fridays they liked to go out. To her, it was difficult enough trying to do this job while taking care of a family, and when her husband was in a sour mood it was impossible.

As she sat in the conference room impatiently waiting for the meeting to begin, she recalled a conversation with Michael about this. He said that the four o'clock meetings didn't make sense to him either, at first. He assumed that Chief Divine wanted to make sure that nobody left early for the weekend. But after meeting on Fridays for a while, Michael decided that it was, in fact, a good way of winding down—a way to take a deep breath at the end of the week, to see what they've done, and to clearly focus on where to start the next week. Besides, he said, it was an opportunity for some of them to plan to go out together for drinks afterward. Julia figured it was for that last reason that it made sense to Michael, but that didn't work for her.

But this was a good day. She was happy to attend the Friday meeting because she wanted to share the new information in the truck scandal that she knew would make Chief Divine let up the pressure on her. Around the long mahogany table in the conference room were all six of the attorneys in the Fraud Division, their law clerks and interns, with Chief Divine at the head. Divine regularly started the meeting with any news he felt he should share from the head office, usually involving big cases that were being tried in the other divisions, or personnel matters. Sometimes he'd share information from the Washington DC Justice Department as well. Then they'd go around the table updating each other on their cases and talking about the legal issues involved. The sharing was helpful to coordinate their efforts and to get feedback on legal precedent and theories that were being used to support the charges.

Sometimes there wasn't much to tell, and this week was like that, except for Julia. She was the second one up and reported on her meeting with Joe Cooper, sharing the information he proffered for a reduction in charges. Just before the meeting, she'd received a phone call from FBI Agent Turkel, who said the sting was planned for Saturday the twenty-seventh, tomorrow. Joe Cooper was to meet with the deputy mayor at one o'clock at the Taste of Chicago, in front of Buckingham Fountain. She planned to be in the office on Sunday to go over the transcripts of the tape, and if the information proved valid, she would prepare to file indictments early the following week. Chief Divine was clearly impressed with this turn of events, and Julia beamed.

Chapter 23

The angelic hosts sang songs of courage and strength to Joe. He would need plenty of both to hold onto his faith while facing the consequences of his sins. The most important thing to the Creator—always—was for the children to find their way back, to remember who they really are, regardless of the outcome. The Angels trusted the Creator to work things out, usually in ways that even they could not expect. They sensed the Creator's mysterious ways underfoot and stood ready to assist.

Reconciliation

After setting the meeting with Clarence, Joe's next job was to see if he could fix the mess he made with Pastor Keith, so he made a call to Pastor Rowland.

Monique answered with her normal efficiency.

"Hello, Monique. How are you today?"

"I'm blessed, Mr. Cooper. How are you?"

"I'm blessed, too." Joe laughed at being able to say that and mean it. "I'm hoping Pastor Rowland is available for just a minute."

"You really must be blessed, because he's in." Monique laughed with him. "I'll see if he's available."

Joe was surprised that Pastor Rowland came on the line so quickly.

"Joe, my friend. What can I do for you today?"

"Pastor, I hope all is well with you."

"Yes, Joe, as well as can be expected. And with you?"

"Just fine, Pastor. I have an amazing story to tell you."

The pastor was completely surprised when Joe told him that Pastor Keith had laid hands on him and helped him to see the error of his ways.

"Well, Joe." He paused. "I really don't know what to say." He paused again and cleared his throat. "I need to think about what this means."

Rowland seemed, for the first time to Joe, at a loss for words. Joe went on. "And I'm sure you'll agree with me that Keith really is an asset to the church. I'd hate to see him go."

Rowland again hesitated before responding. "I understand. Joe, as you can see, this has taken me by surprise. But it surely is a blessing. Let me see what I can do."

Joe thought that was about all he'd be able to get out of Pastor Rowland at this point. "Thank you Pastor, for listening and considering my request." As he hung up, Joe felt like his heart was singing within him. He tried to describe how he felt to himself, and the only word he could come up with was "lighter." He felt less burdened than he had felt in years.

Joe then decided to invite Kenisha and Pastor Keith to dinner that evening. He wanted Kenisha to know that he had worked out a deal. He was pleasantly surprised when they both agreed to meet him at the Calypso Restaurant in Hyde Park, at 7:30 PM.

Joe arrived at seven fifteen. The Calypso had a relaxed, Caribbean theme with good food and drinks. When Joe and Kenisha were dating, they came here often. They both liked the jerk chicken and key lime pie. On the way over, Joe had stopped by a florist on Fifty-fifth Street and picked up a bouquet of roses for Kenisha, nice ones this time. They seated him at a back corner table while he waited for Keith and Kenisha to arrive.

Keith got there first. Joe stood up to shake his hand and grinned broadly. "Hey, Pastor Keith. It's good to see you. I'm glad you could come."

"I'm glad to see you, too, Joe. It really is good to see you." He emphasized the "good" as he shook Joe's hand solidly and searched his eyes sincerely. They both just smiled at each other; no more words were necessary.

As Keith was sitting, Kenisha arrived at the table. They both stood and smiled, saying at the same time, "Kenisha."

She greeted them without smiling. "Hello, Pastor Keith. Hello, Joe."

Joe continued to smile. He leaned toward her as if he was going to give her a kiss. It was a movement that flowed naturally from his joy at seeing her, but he quickly thought better and pulled back. He helped her with her chair and handed her the roses. He wasn't quite sure how to handle her unexpressive "Thank you."

They agreed on a Riesling to start their meal. When the waiter left to get the wine, Joe explained to Kenisha and Keith, "I wanted to treat you two to dinner tonight so I could let you know that I'm living up to my promise to Kenisha. I met with the Assistant U.S. Attorney today. If everything goes as planned, I'll pay my debt to the public and won't have to do any time."

Kenisha reacted with a controlled, tight smile. "That's good news, Joe. I'm glad it looks like it's going to work out." Joe was happy that he got even a little smile out of her.

Keith also encouraged him. "Good work, buddy. Will you have to wear a wire or anything like that?"

Joe frowned. "I can't really talk about it anymore. But I'll be okay. You don't have to worry. I just want you two to know that I'm living up to what I said. I want to thank you for all you've done for me." He turned to look at Kenisha. "And for putting up with me through it all."

She smiled tightly again.

After the waiter brought the Riesling and poured their drinks, Joe held up his wineglass. "A toast to a brighter future."

Both Keith and Kenisha held up their glasses in response. "Hear, hear."

After they ordered their meals, Joe turned to Keith. "Pastor Keith, I also want you to know that I've called Pastor Rowland and told him how you saved my life. I told him that I really admire you and that it would be a blessing to me if you were to continue to work at the church.

I don't know if it will help, but Pastor Rowland really did seem pleased when he found out how you helped me."

Keith's response was unexpected. "Thanks for that, Joe. But, believe it or not, now that I've had a few days to think about it, I'm convinced that God may have other plans for me. You know that God has this way of making us pay attention, don't you? Getting fired has made me pay more attention to what God may be calling me to do." He took a sip of wine before going on. "I've been looking around to see if there are any churches looking for pastors. All I ask for you to do is to pray that God will lead me to where God wants me to be, sooner rather than later."

"Hear, hear," Joe said, as they lifted their glasses again.

Kenisha was mostly quiet during dinner. She was still trying to take it all in. Joe had all the outward makings of a perfect husband. And if he truly had found Christ in his life, then she would be foolish not to take him back. As Kenisha sat there watching Joe and Keith, it dawned on her that in spite of all of the pain and heartbreak that Joe brought into her life, he had always been a good father to Kisha, and Kisha really loved him. That realization made her almost clear that letting Joe back in her life would be the right thing to do; for them to be together as a family would be best for Kisha. But somewhere deep within, that old feeling that there was something not quite right was still there. Something she couldn't quite put her finger on, couldn't quite express. She struggled to suppress it, ashamed to admit even to herself that she kind of enjoyed the idea of being free.

Chapter 24

The Opposers felt their enemies' resignation to defeat and roiled in derisive sounds that mimicked laughter. But they had too many painful memories with their enemies to become complacent. They knew that events could move in unexpected directions, and so they continued to watch these two closely and to intervene as necessary.

A Beautiful Day

Michael thought his head was going to fall off. The rude and insistent alarm clock set off in it a painful, rhythmic beating. He fumbled around until he found the switch and turned the radio alarm off. It was 7:00 AM. His brain refused to function for him. He couldn't remember what day it was or what it was that he was supposed to be doing. As he lay there, the fog slowly began to lift. He looked at the calendar on the nightstand, which informed him that it was Saturday, June 26. He'd forgotten to turn the alarm off last night. Thank God for Saturdays! He rolled over to go back to sleep, only to find his latest bar date smiling in his face. He tried to remember her name. She had short, red hair and a freckled face that was familiar, but that was all his brain was registering.

"Ohhhh, my head. Hi, baby, you're still here." It wasn't the most romantic thing to say, but he was still trying to turn his mind on.

"Yes, Michael." She slid over next to him. "Remember, you said you wanted to spend the whole weekend with me. You said we'd do something romantic today." She reached for him under the sheets. "And I can't think of a more romantic way to start the day than to continue where we left off last night." She turned her body over to face him, angling to move on top.

That woke him up. "Hey, yes. Hmmmm. I said that?" Michael slipped out of her grip and sat up, a little too fast. The snare drum in his head went off again. "Look, I really wish I could do that. That was wishful thinking on my part. But I've got some work in the office I have to do, or my ass is grass. I'm sorry, baby, but I've got to go."

She moved over to the other side of the bed and pouted while still trying to look sweet. "Well, I know your work is important, so I'll let you off this time."

"Annie." He was glad he finally remembered her name. She was one of the bartenders at the tavern the attorneys in the office went to for drinks after dinner yesterday. "Annie, baby, we'll have to do this another time, okay?" He gave her a kiss, got up, offered her a towel, showed her where the shower was, and gave her a smack on her behind to let her know that he still cared. "That's a good girl."

Michael ambled into the kitchen and took an Alka-Seltzer to turn off the drum in his head. He made some coffee and gave some to Annie when she came out of the shower. After sending her off, he showered and put on some blue jeans. He then opened the blinds and realized for the first time that the sun was shining brightly. The fact that it was a beautiful day helped him to decide that he really did need to go into the office. He threw on a wrinkled T-shirt and headed out the door. As the cool and refreshing air hit him, he marveled at how beautiful the day felt. Yet it made him feel lonely. He would like to have someone who he really wanted to spend a day like this with, someone who was more interesting to him than his work.

The ride downtown on the brown line only took a few minutes. He looked at his watch. It was only nine-thirty. He thought he could get a lot done this morning, and then he'd get some lunch and come back home to pull out his bike to see if it needed fixing. He'd take it to the shop and hopefully ride over to the lakeshore later that day. He stopped by a Starbucks near the office and picked up a Grande Mocha, his favorite, and a blueberry muffin for breakfast.

Michael showed his identification, said a friendly greeting to the security guard, and then headed up to his office. He was surprised to find that there was no one there; he'd usually find a few attorneys around and sometimes the law clerks or interns. He guessed the day was too beautiful but was glad that he wouldn't have distractions. He went into the office and shut the door in case anybody else came in who might want to talk. He was still feeling lonely, but not for the company of anyone who might come into the office. He turned on his computer and buried himself in his brief writing.

Kisha woke up both Essie and Kenisha at about seven on Saturday morning. They all helped to make pancakes, eggs, sausage, fresh sliced peaches and orange juice for breakfast. It was a beautiful, bright, late June day. One of Chicago's best, Kenisha thought as she opened the sliding doors to the deck off the kitchen. The slightly cool and refreshingly clear air caressed her skin gently, while the sunshine was just warm enough to let her know it was there. Kenisha felt as if the day was inviting them to enjoy outside. It lifted her spirit. She thought about the dinner with Joe last night, and she began to have new hope about a happy family. She thought she really could forgive him. She really could. She smiled to herself and said thank you to God for helping Joe and her, too.

The bright, clear day energized Kisha. She jumped up and down the deck stairs in her pajamas counting them out loud. Kenisha opened Friday's weekend edition of the *Sun-Times* to read as she relaxed on the deck with her mother and a second cup of coffee. "Oh, look. Today's the twenty-sixth. I forgot the Taste starts this weekend. Would you two like to go down this afternoon for a while?"

Kisha responded with an excited "Yes!" even though she didn't know what the "Taste" was.

Essie begged off. "It's just too many people for me. Besides, I need to go home, take care of my house, and do some laundry. I have to bake a cake for the Sunday school graduate's reception tomorrow. Why don't you two just go on without me?"

"Are you sure? It's a beautiful day, Mom. I'd love to have you come with us." Kenisha was enjoying the bonding between her and her mother. She felt like they were really becoming friends.

Essie was relaxing on the lounge chair in a housecoat over her pajamas. "Yes, I'm sure, sweetie. I would feel better if I could take care of some things now, to get ready for next week. You two enjoy yourselves. I need to be home for a while."

"Okay, Mom." Kenisha knew that her mother wanted to get back home after staying with them all week. She turned to her daughter. "Kisha, Gramma and I are going to clean up the kitchen. You go into your playroom and put away your toys from last night. Then we'll get ready to go. Okay?"

"Okay, Mommy." Kisha ran downstairs, excited to have a reason to clean up her playthings.

Kenisha looked at her watch. It was about ten o'clock. She thought they ought to be able to get there by noon, and then they'd decide what they'd have for lunch and stay until time for Kisha's nap. They rushed around cleaning up and getting dressed to go. By the time they left the house, it was eleven thirty, and in the rush Kenisha left her cell phone charging on the kitchen counter.

Agent Turkel's office was in a complex of federal buildings on Roosevelt Road near Twenty-first Street. Joe turned into the circular parking lot and walked over to the guard house adjacent to the lot. There he was directed to the building with the address Turkel had given him. He walked through security to the reception office in that building.

"I'm here to see Agent Turkel." Joe spoke through a circular opening of a glass window. The receptionist pointed him to a sign-in sheet, which he signed as she put a call through to the agent. It was about eleven forty-five; Joe was early. He thought he could get through this. He knew Harding well enough that he didn't think there should be any suspicion on his part. He told himself this should be a piece of cake, but he recognized the tension in himself.

Agent Turkel came out of a set of double doors, and with him was Agent Martinez. Agent Turkel was tall, not heavy but with a beer belly. His slightly balding blond hair with the mustache and goatee made Joe think he was in his late thirties or early forties. Agent Martinez was shorter, darker, and more fit, neatly trimmed. Joe figured he was the lower in rank between these two because Turkel always seemed to take the lead. They ushered him into a small conference room near the entry of the hallway and shut the door.

"Take off your shirt. Let's get this on you." Agent Martinez put a strap around Joe's chest with a mini-microphone right in the middle of his chest. He then handed him a small earpiece. Agent Turkel explained, "The mic strapped around your chest is connected wirelessly to a receiver that we'll have in a truck about one hundred yards from the fountain. We'll be able to hear and record everything both you and Harding are saying. The earpiece fits into your ear so that you can hear us, if we need you to ask anything more specific, or if you have any questions. Let's test it out."

Martinez pushed some buttons on the recorder and nodded at Joe to talk. Joe couldn't think of anything but "Testing, testing, one-two-three, testing."

Martinez pushed a few more buttons and replayed it. "Working fine," he said briefly. "Put the earpiece in your ear, nice and snug."

After Joe put it in, Martinez whispered something almost inaudibly that Joe heard clearly. "I hear you, loud and clear." Joe was surprised at how powerful the little ear device was.

"What's your plan, Joe? I mean, how are you going to get Harding to admit his involvement out loud?" Agent Turkel asked.

"I'm going to tell him that his buddy who collects the money from me has been taking more than the usual and to tell him to lighten up some. I want him to think that Moe is taking a bigger cut than he's aware of."

Turkel smiled an unfriendly smile. "Good idea. That ought to get him to admit he's involved. You need to get him to implicate who Moe works for. Why don't you ask him to let you go to Moe's boss?"

"Listen, Agent Turkel, I told you I would turn over Harding, and not anybody else. I don't want to get my head blown off. It's not my job to find out who the mob connection is. I'm giving you Clarence Harding. You can pressure him to talk about his connection." Joe was shaken by the request.

"Okay, okay. I was just trying to make the most out of all this effort. There, it's all set. When we've got all we need, we'll let you know. You can send your friend Harding off and meet us back in the office later this afternoon. We don't want Harding to see you with us, so don't come to the truck." He patted Joe on the back. "There's nothing to worry about with this one. Harding doesn't know a thing, and we don't expect anything to happen to you. It's a piece of cake."

Joe went outside, lit a cigarette with shaking hands, and got into his car. He thought about what kind of piece of cake this was—setting up a friend so that he could save his own ass. The thought kicked him into soberness about the seriousness of what he was doing. He was going to have to start all over from scratch. He could be blackballed from government work, out of a job, and labeled a traitor. He wondered if he could really make it in Chicago after all of this.

He thought about those papers that gave him ownership of the company. They were accurate and quite legal—they were not sham documents. What they had done on paper was legal, even if their agreed-upon behavior was not. He would check with his attorney about that. Maybe it was time he used what he was taught in management school and really take over the company. He'd have to keep the company's name clear of the mob connection for that to work. A glimmer of hope encouraged him to keep going.

He drove back to the Palmer House, left the car there, and walked over to Grant Park to the Taste of Chicago. It was about twelve forty-five.

Chapter 25

Both the angelic hosts and the Opposers felt the intensity building in the Creator's plan. They knew when the Creator's hand was moving. All they could do was stay ready and move into action when the time was right. The angelic hosts sang down songs of love and courage. The Opposers sent out waves of fear, deceit, and confusion. None of them knew just how it would work out; they only knew that it would be soon.

Mysterious Ways

Roger Cheatem, an assistant secretary who had been in the U.S. Attorney's office for about six months working mainly for Michael, came to the office a little before twelve that afternoon. He went into the outer office of the suite where Michael was working. In his brief survey of the office, he didn't notice that Michael's light was on under the door, just that all the doors were shut and the office was quiet. Satisfied that there was no one there, he went into the conference room, got down on his knees, and reached under to the middle of the long table to pull out a small recording device, no larger than a cigarette lighter, that he had attached there early on Friday. He stashed it in his pocket and quickly hurried out. Back in the office suite, he shut the outer office door and wound back the recorder to the beginning of the taped meeting. He fast-forwarded through it until he got to the part he wanted, and then he listened to Julia's report at the staff meeting. He then speed-dialed his cell phone.

"Cooper's singing. He's wearing a wire. Yeah, he's meeting Harding this afternoon at 1:00 PM. At Buckingham Fountain. Yeah, that's right, today at one o'clock." Cheatem shut the phone off and started packing his backpack to leave.

Michael heard the door to the outer office when it first opened. He stayed quiet, not wanting to be disturbed. Then he heard it shut, and in a few minutes open and shut again. He thought it might be one of the attorneys, but he didn't hear any other office doors in their suite being opened. He heard voices that sounded muffled, stopping and starting. That made him curious enough to put his ear to his door and listen. He heard Cheatem's phone conversation loud and clear then, and he realized that what he heard before was a tape recording. He immediately opened his door.

Cheatem was putting the recorder in his satchel when Michael's door opened. He stopped, looking at Michael wide-eyed with fear.

Michael shouted, "What the hell are you doing?"

Cheatem, caught off guard, threw the backpack on his shoulder and opened the outer office door, but Michael grabbed the backpack and turned Cheatem around. Without thinking what he was doing, Michael hit Cheatem solidly with an uppercut to the left side of his jaw. Cheatem fell backward, all of the contents coming out of the unfastened backpack.

"Get up." Cheatem was short and thin, no match for Michael. He didn't resist when Michael grabbed his shirt and stood him up. "What are you doing? Who were you calling? Who do you work for?"

Cheatem held his hands protectively in front of his face. "Don't hit me. I was just doing what I was told. I don't know anything," he whined.

"You tell me what you know or I'll beat the living daylights out of you. Why were you taping our meeting? Who put you up to it?" He couldn't just ask one question at a time.

"I was asked to do it by someone who helped me get this job. He told me to tape the staff meetings and to report back to him." Cheatem sobbed. He didn't take pain well.

"Who asked you?" Michael lifted him up by the front of his shirt with his fist ready to swing again.

"Brian McArthur. My friend's name is Brian McArthur." Cheatem was shaking.

"Who the hell is Brian McArthur, and why does he want you to record our staff meetings?" Michael was getting impatient with this sniveling bastard.

"He works ... he works in Clarence Harding's office. He's a special assistant to the deputy mayor. That's how he got me the job."

"Who was that you called?"

"It was Brian."

Michael let him go. Cheatem fell back on the desk behind him. Michael picked up the desk phone and dialed security, standing over Cheatem until the guard came. After Michael told the guard what had happened, the guard handcuffed Cheatem and said he would hold him until the police came.

Michael was frantic. If Harding knew that Joe was singing to the Feds, who knew what he'd do. Harding had a lot to lose, and he would be facing a lot of jail time. It wouldn't be enough for Harding to try to clear himself while talking to Joe. Joe knew too much. The mob would do away with Joe just because he was singing, whether Harding could be convicted or not. And not the least of Michael's angst was the thought that he had made all this happen, trying to protect Kenisha. If Joe got hurt, he would blame himself for hurting her rather than helping her.

The best thing to do would be to call Joe directly. Michael looked up Kenisha's name in his BlackBerry and realized that all he had was her office number. He called the hospital to see if she was working, but she was not. He told them it was an emergency, and the secretary on duty, remembering him, gave him her home and cell phone numbers. No answer at those, either. He couldn't remember her mother's name or her church. He called the FBI office to see if he could reach someone who knew about the sting, but there was no answer there. He thought about calling Julia, but it was twelve forty-five now, and he knew by the time they were able to find anybody who knew anything, it'd be too late. He decided to go himself.

Michael ran down five floors to the exit on Dearborn, not wanting to wait for the slow elevator. He headed south to Jackson Boulevard.

Just as he was cutting across the driveway of a parking garage near the corner of Jackson and Adams, a large truck came barreling down the ramp. The driver honked his horn and screeched the tires, but it was too late. A bystander screamed. Michael turned and saw the truck about to hit him … and then it was on the other side of him. He stopped and looked around and saw the truck past him, at the end of the drive at the stop sign, the driver shouting obscenities at Michael through the open window.

"How in the hell …" Michael didn't have time to think about it more than that. He got over to Jackson and ran and pushed his way through the busy streets over to Grant Park.

Kenisha and Kisha had a lunch of pizza and ribs at a table in an eating area off the main pathway. Not particularly healthy, but it was fun for both of them. Then they waited in line to get ice-cream cones and were eating them as they navigated through the crowd. Kenisha hadn't been to a Taste of Chicago in quite a few years and had forgotten how crowded it could get. She held Kisha's hand tightly. "Everybody and their mother is here on this nice day," she mumbled to herself.

The crowds were intimidating. The people moved in packed groups, like schools of fish, each facing in different directions. In order to go against the group trajectory, Kenisha had to navigate with Kisha in front, pushing their way through. It was too much for a child as young as Kisha. So Kenisha moved out of the larger crowd and headed south to Buckingham Fountain, where she thought there would be more room to sit for a few minutes, and possibly a Porta-Potty to use before heading home. Besides, Kisha had never seen the beautiful fountain close up.

As they neared the fountain, Kisha twisted her hand out of Kenisha's, shouting "Daddy!" and ran through the thinning crowd. Kenisha looked up and saw Joe standing alone by the fountain. "Kisha!" She didn't want her running loose even for a minute and ran after her. Joe hadn't seen either of them yet. He was smoking a cigarette and looked like he was waiting for somebody. Kisha got there first, grabbed him by the leg, and dropped her ice-cream cone. "Hi, baby, what are you doing here?" He hugged her, looked up, and saw Kenisha headed toward him, too. "Kenisha, what are you doing here?"

Michael desperately pushed his way through the crowd. When he got near the fountain he saw them all there. He stopped about twenty feet away. He didn't expect to see Kenisha and Kisha there. As he tried to figure out what to say to them, he saw a man in a dark jacket about ten feet directly in front of him with his hand in his pocket, with what looked like the muzzle of a gun sticking up through the jacket, pointing at Joe and his family. Michael shot forward and screamed, "Joe, Joe, watch out! Joe, get down, get down!"

Joe turned toward the voice and automatically pushed Kenisha behind him to protect her and Kisha. Just as he moved, the first bullet hit him directly in the chest. The muzzled gun barely made a noise. Kenisha reflexively bent over to cover Kisha as more bullets flew and blood spurted out of Joe's chest. Pop, pop, pop, pop! Both Joe and Kenisha dropped to the ground. Kisha screamed.

The crowd burst into madness, screaming and running. The gunman had counted on that, turning to run with the crowd back into anonymity, but instead he ran right into Michael, who was coming at him. He raised his gun, but it was too late. Michael tackled him to the ground as the gun went off again in the air. Catching him by surprise, Michael was able to hit him and wrestle the gun away from him. He held him down until the police arrived.

A woman saw Kisha crying and went over to move her away from her mother and father, trying to keep her from seeing the blood that was pooling around them. She tried to comfort her. A policeman on horseback was the first one to arrive. He called for backup and tended to Joe and Kenisha. Within three minutes Turkel and Martinez were there and took over custody of the gunman. Michael went over to see about Joe and Kenisha, then he retrieved Kisha, telling her that he was a friend of her mother's. He held her tightly.

Just a few minutes later an ambulance made it through the crowd. Soon the grounds were teeming with FBI, police, ambulances, and curiosity seekers. The police took a statement from Michael. Joe and Kenisha were quickly triaged and taken to Northwestern Memorial Hospital. Michael went with Kisha to the hospital by police car, and he stayed with her until Essie arrived.

Chapter 26

The Angels rejoiced with great songs of celebration! They were absolutely delighted to greet the spirit called Joe back into their realm and to have him sing with them with total and complete joy and thanksgiving. He realized how close he had come to being lost. With great jubilation and love, the Creator welcomed this precious spirit back.

They continued to see to Kenisha and Michael. Joe helped them sing down songs of healing and forgiveness.

Aftershock

Kenisha was still in ICU when she awoke to see her mother standing over her. Essie's eyes were shut, her mouth silently working and her hands folded in prayer.

"Mom." Kenisha tried to focus.

"Kenisha. Oh, thank God. Thank God." Essie looked at her with tears in her eyes.

As the fog began to lift, Kenisha started to remember. "Kisha! Where is Kisha?" She struggled to sit up but couldn't move her right arm.

Essie placed a calming hand on the arm not attached to the tubes. "Kenisha, she's fine. She's fine. The police brought her here from the park. When I got here I made sure she was all right and called Connie, who came and picked her up. She's going to spend the night there, and I'll get her in the morning."

After breathing a sigh of relief, Kenisha said, "Joe?"

Essie's tears fell. She hesitated for a couple of seconds, as if deciding how much she would tell. She breathed deeply and then shook her head when she said, "He didn't make it, honey. He didn't make it. He died trying to protect you and Kisha."

Kenisha was surprised at how quickly the tears started falling when she heard that. She didn't know what to say. "Why?"

"I don't know. The lawyer from the U.S. Attorney's Office was here with Kisha when I got here. He's the one you told me about, who told Joe to turn himself in. He was at the park, too, and the police told me that he tackled the shooter. The police said that it may have been a mob hit. But they didn't know any more."

"Oh no. Oh nooooo." Kenisha moaned. "It's all my fault. It's all my fault, Mom. I'm the one who told him to do it."

Essie took charge. "Kenisha. Kenisha!" She made Kenisha look at her. "Listen to me, Kenisha. I don't know much about all of this, but what I do know is that it's not your fault. There's nothing you could have said or done that would have caused that man to try to shoot you and your husband. You were shot, too, weren't you? Don't you start beating yourself up over this. You did not pull that trigger. Do you hear me?"

Kenisha didn't respond; she knew better than to argue when her mother was like this. The doctor came in then and told her that they had removed a bullet from her right arm, that one bullet had grazed her side but did not hit any organs, and that another grazed her head. Other than some scars, she would recover completely. Kenisha knew that wasn't true.

Essie stayed with Kenisha until she was moved from emergency into a room on the fourth floor and she was sedated to sound sleep.

On Sunday morning, Pastor Keith came to Kenisha's room at about 10:00 AM. Essie was there, sitting near the bed. She got up to greet him and then motioned him to sit. "I'm going to get a cup of coffee," she said as she left.

"Hi, Kenisha." Keith was dressed casually in a short-sleeved knit shirt and slacks. His face registered concern. "I came as soon as I heard.

How are you feeling?" He sat in the chair next to the bed, where Essie had been sitting.

Kenisha was sitting up. Her head was bandaged around the top, her right arm was in a sling, and she was connected to the usual IV lines. She and Essie had been watching one of those Sunday morning talk shows, but she hadn't really been listening to it.

She clicked it off when Keith sat down. "I'm a little woozy from the pain medicine, but they tell me I'll be okay. I look worse than I feel. Two bullets grazed me, and the other was in my arm, but it didn't hit any major veins or arteries or anything. The doctor said this morning that they might release me later today."

Keith breathed a sigh of relief and took her hand. "Thank God for that." He sat there with her for a few minutes, just holding her hand. "I'm so sorry about Joe."

Kenisha looked at him with pain in her eyes. She couldn't say anything.

He used his comforting voice. "You know, Kenisha, we can never tell why some things happen. God's ways are sometimes just mysterious to us. And, yes, sometimes what seem like bad things really do happen to good people. Our faith calls us to know and believe that somehow, in some way, it all will work out for good. Joe was good people, Kenisha." He looked at her intensely, wanting to make sure that she'd hear what he was saying.

Kenisha tried to speak, but all she could say was "He had changed …" before sobbing.

Keith squeezed her hand a bit. "Joe was good people. We know that he turned his life around in time, so now we know that he's with God. Why God decided he wanted him to come home right now is not something we can second-guess. It's nobody's fault that this happened. Joe's life was saved when he confessed his sins and tried to do what was right. You were a part of that process, but you were not in any way responsible for his death. Do you hear me, Kenisha?" His voice was sincere and healing.

She did not respond.

"Do you hear me, Kenisha?" Pastor Keith insisted.

"Yes, Pastor Keith. But if I hadn't made him go talk to the prosecutor, he never would have gotten shot. Everybody is telling me it's not my fault, but I know that if it hadn't been for me, this never would have happened." Her eyes pleaded with him to make some sense of it for her.

Keith looked her squarely in the eyes. "You don't really know that, do you, Kenisha? Joe's involvement with the mob is one of the things he wanted to straighten out when he decided to turn his life around. That was his decision. You had some information that helped him, but he had already planned to do it before you told him about that attorney. What I can tell you for sure is that because he cooperated with them, his name and your family's name won't get dragged through the mud of that trial." Keith continued to hold her hand.

Kenisha wanted to believe it, but Joe's death still felt like a weight on her. "Yes, Pastor Keith" was all she could muster. After a few moments, she smiled a little. "Do you have something for me to read that will help me through all of this?"

Keith grinned. "I sure do." He opened his Bible and started reading from Matthew 8:23–27, the story about Jesus calming the storm that had caused the disciples to be afraid, and how he told them they needed more faith. "Sometimes we have storms and troubles in our lives to test our faith, Kenisha. I don't know why Joe had to die, but our job is to hang on to Jesus and our faith even more strongly. If we truly believe that Joe is safely with the Lord, then we can't grieve but for so long over him, because we know he's in the better place. Our job is to keep on believing that all that is done will work out for good in the end, especially when we can't see what that end will be."

Kenisha's tears started to flow again. "I do believe, Pastor Keith. I was so happy that Joe found his way back to God. I had hoped that we might have the kind of marriage and family life I'd always wanted, so I guess I'm crying over that, too." She sobbed silently for a moment and then wiped her eyes and blew her nose. "I really do believe that Joe is okay now. I'm so glad that God saved him. That's the important thing. I'll miss him, but I'll see him again, too, won't I?"

Keith smiled again. "Yes, you certainly will, Kenisha. You'll see him again one day—but not too soon, I hope. That's the good news that Jesus came to make happen. We're all going home one day. And knowing that means that we can get through everything that happens in this world, because we already have the victory."

Kenisha smiled at that. She already knew it, but she needed to hear it again. It warmed her heart and took away some of her pain and guilt. "Thank you, Pastor Keith, thank you." She wiped her eyes again.

"Kenisha, you're always welcome. You'll need some time to heal, both physically and spiritually, so make sure you get plenty of rest and do what the doctors tell you. And remember to look at this story and meditate on it and what it means for your life right now. Would you like to pray with me now?"

"Yes, Pastor Keith. I'd like that very much."

Essie returned shortly after Keith left. She stayed until after Kenisha had lunch and then left to get some things for Kenisha to wear when discharged. A little later, around 1:00 PM, Kenisha heard a gentle knock on the door. Michael peaked his head in, then entered. "Kenisha?" he said, hesitantly.

"Hello, Michael." She looked at him without expression.

"I brought you some flowers." He pulled from behind his back a beautiful and rich bouquet.

"Please put them over on the windowsill." She wasn't sure how she felt about seeing Michael.

"I'm glad to see you're awake. How're you feeling?" He sat in the chair on the opposite wall, not the one closest to the bed.

"I'm doing okay, Michael. This turban isn't just for beauty purposes, though. One shot grazed my head, one grazed my side, and the other hit me in the right arm. Nothing serious, though. I should be going home later today." Her words were perfunctory and emotionless.

Michael smiled a bit. "Thank goodness. I'm glad it isn't any more serious than that. But I'm really sorry you got hurt." He hesitated for a moment and then looked into her eyes. "I'm really sorry, Kenisha, about Joe, too. I never meant for this to happen."

"I know you didn't want this to happen, Michael, but couldn't you have provided some better protection for Joe? You knew the mob was involved in this. How could you just let him go out there all by himself?" She found herself getting worked up without meaning to. Somewhere inside she knew she shouldn't blame Michael, but she couldn't help it right now.

He stood up and came a little closer. "Joe told us that Harding was an old pal of his, and taping the conversation between two friends was supposed to be pretty straightforward. I'm not trying to make excuses, because I take all the blame for it, Kenisha. I really do. But what happened is that the mob put a mole in our office, and they found out that Joe was talking to us. I tried to stop it. I really did try to stop it as soon as I found out. That's why I was there. I didn't know until right before it was supposed to go down and …" He paused and took a breath, his eyes full of pain. "I couldn't stop it. I'm so sorry, Kenisha. I'm really so sorry."

He looked like his heart was going to break. She knew that he was telling the truth, but it didn't make her feel better about it. She remained silent, just looking at him with flat, emotionless eyes, refusing to respond to the pain in his eyes.

"Look, maybe I shouldn't have come here. I don't want you to be upset. I just wanted you to know that we arrested the shooter and the guy who set up the shooting. We couldn't have done it without Joe." Michael hesitated for a moment, searching for something in her eyes. He looked forlorn as he said, "I'm sorry for your loss, Kenisha. I won't bother you anymore."

Kenisha turned her head away from him.

As he walked out the door, Michael's shoulders slumped.

Chapter 27

Even the angelic hosts can be amazed at how the Creator wields love with such intricate attention to detail in order to bring a part of the Plan together. No matter how difficult and messy situations seem to the children, the Creator always can turn them to serve the Creator's purposes. The Creator knows how difficult it is for the children to remember who they are when they enter the created realm. The Creator never leaves them alone, constantly calls them to remember, and intervenes through the angelic forces to help them.

Healing

"Do you think I should wear a hat, Mom?" Kenisha and Essie stood in the front room of Kenisha's home, waiting for the limousine that was to take them to the church for the funeral service for Joe. Kenisha wore a simple black V-neck, A-line dress with a short-sleeved jacket, accentuated by a single strand of pearls and black silk stockings. She wore low-heeled black pumps and carried a small black silk purse.

Essie was dressed in a simple black suit and white blouse, and she had on a broad-brimmed black straw hat with a white flower on the brim. "Yes, I do, Kenisha."

"The only one I have is this small one." She held up a plain, small round black straw hat. "It doesn't have a veil or anything. I should have bought one." It was Friday, six days after the shooting. Her head bandage was just a patch now, and her arm was wrapped but no longer in a sling.

"It's fine. The pillbox look suits you."

Kenisha looked at herself in the hall mirror as she put the hat on. She could still see signs of the bruises Joe inflicted on her around her left eye. It was hard to believe that happened less than two weeks ago. "What about gloves?"

Essie looked at her daughter with concern. "You don't have to wear gloves, Kenisha. Do you really have gloves, anyway?"

"Well, I don't, but I thought we could get some if we needed them."

Essie moved to put an arm around her daughter. "It's okay, baby, we're going to get through this." Just then Kisha came into the room, dressed in a fluffy white chiffon dress, girded with a pink cummerbund and pink flower, white shoes and socks, and a small-brimmed white hat.

"Don't you look beautiful, darling." Kenisha bent down and gave her a big hug.

"Mommy, are you going to cry again?" Kisha looked at her with big, tearful eyes.

This child sensed Kenisha's emotions even when she was trying her best not to show them. Kisha's empathy always helped Kenisha to pull it together. "Not now, baby. Not now. Come on, it's time for us to go. Do you want to take Miss Sally with you?"

"Yes." Kisha smiled and ran to get her favorite doll.

Essie went out the door, picked up the *Sun-Times*, and looked at the headline: "Hired Truck Scandal Hits the Skids." She showed it to Kenisha, who took it and scanned it.

"Well, I do thank God that they were able to keep Joe and AAA out of the scandal. I do thank God for that." Kenisha seemed relieved. The limousine pulled up, and as they went out to it, they each held one of Kisha's hands while she jumped along, safely between them.

Keith was grateful that David Rowland had called to invite him to participate in Joe Cooper's funeral. When Keith arrived at the church about a half hour before the funeral, David sent an usher to ask Keith to meet with him alone for a few minutes. Keith took the stairs up to the third floor. When he entered the office, Monique came from around the desk, gave him a hug, and told him that Pastor Rowland was waiting for him. Keith knocked.

"Come in." David came from behind his desk and greeted Keith with his hand out. He was already in his clerical robes, ready for the funeral. "Keith, Joe called me the day before he was killed to tell me what had happened to him when you were with him. What an amazing blessing that was!" David smiled as he continued to shake Keith's hand.

Keith responded warily, "Yes, David, God is still in the miracle business and shows up to prove that to us every once in a while." He removed his hand from the handshake.

David smiled and patted him on the back. "I want to thank you for your part in that. And I want to apologize for acting hastily over that divorce thing." David hesitated and cleared his throat. "Joe wanted me to know that you were helping to patch things up with him and Kenisha and that he'd like to see you back on the staff here." He paused, searching Keith's eyes. "How about it?"

Keith winced. "Pastor Rowland, I appreciate your offer. I really do. But in this last week I've done a lot of meditating and praying. And I'm sure that God had the two of us go through all of that to help me see some new possibilities for ministry. I know now that there's a new ministry waiting for me. And I've decided to trust God enough to try to let that happen."

David didn't stop smiling, but he took his hand off Keith's shoulder. "Well, you know that if you come back, you can grow your new ministry and not have to worry about keeping afloat. I know that it's tough making ends meet when you're starting out." David really did seem to want him back.

Keith figured cynically that David must have discovered how much Keith really did around there since he left. "Thank you for offering, David. But you know, I'm sure that God wants me to step out on faith this time, and I'm going to do it. And I've already got some things I'm working on. Thanks, but no thanks." Keith was first to move toward the door.

After the interment, the funeral participants returned to the church for the traditional repast. For a large and important funeral as this, the dedicated women of the church prepared a feast of fried chicken, roast turkey and dressing, potato salad, macaroni and cheese, collard greens, string beans, hot rolls, corn bread, sweet potato and apple pies, and several different kinds of homemade cakes. Pastor Keith lingered at the large round dining table with Kenisha, Essie, Kisha, Joe's aunt, uncle, and nephew, as well as Connie and Mary. Pastor Rowland had only stayed for a few minutes before he had to leave.

As Keith rose to leave, Kenisha rose with him and walked him to the door. "Thank you for helping with everything."

Keith turned as they reached the door. "You know, Kenisha, that I'm available whenever you need to talk."

She nodded and, taking his elbow, she walked with him outside. As they stood outside the door of the church, she said, "Pastor Keith, is there someone who can talk to Kisha, too? She doesn't really understand death just yet, and she misses her daddy. She knows he was hurt like me and wants to know where he is. I told her he's in heaven and can't come back, but I don't think she understands." She took a breath. "And I'm also worried about her being there when we were shot and what that memory may do to her. She's still sleeping in the bed with me now, and I need some help with how to handle her."

"I was wondering if you had found anyone to help counsel you. I have just the person, who I know will be happy to talk to both of you together. She works with me." He gave her a card.

Kenisha read it out loud: "The Reverend Keith Summers, Pastoral Counselor. Christian Counseling Center."

She looked at him and smiled with a gleam in her eye. "What, you've got a new job already?"

He laughed. "Some people I knew in seminary have asked me to work with them while I see what God's got ahead for me. Counseling is one of my gifts, and I believe God wants me to use it more for God's people. It's what I was trained to do, and you know, Kenisha, it feels like the right thing for me." He realized how true that was as he said it, and he beamed. "You know that if you need me, I'll be there, don't you?"

"Yes, Pastor Keith. You're my favorite pastor. You let me know when you're ready to start your new church, and I'll be there with bells on." Keith was happy to see her smile genuinely again.

They hugged. Keith carefully tucked her last words in his heart as he walked to his car.

Chapter 28

Created life is much more limited than the timeless realm of true existence. But sometimes there are advantages in those limitations. One advantage of living where there is a beginning and end to everything is the recognition of change over time. Things do change. And time does heal wounds. The Angels are already rejoicing as they see the Plan unfold.

They Remember

Kenisha was running out the door of the rehab unit, almost late to pick up Kisha for her piano lesson. It was Monday, December 6, and Christmas was approaching faster than she'd expected. She thought she'd take Kisha downtown to look at the Christmas decorations in the store windows. Maybe they'd have dinner out and do a little Christmas shopping before going home. She was thinking about how much she could get done before the snowfall that was predicted for tomorrow, when she almost ran smack into Michael, who was entering.

He looked at her, clearly startled.

"Hello, Michael. It's good to see you again." Kenisha smiled.

"Really?" was all he could say.

He looked different to her than he had before, a little more grown-up, she thought. "Yes. Look, I'd like to talk to you again, but I'm late to pick up Kisha. Can we talk sometime?"

"What, yes, sure ...," He fumbled for words. "How about dinner, I mean lunch. How about lunch sometime this week?"

"That sounds good. Maybe Wednesday?"

"Yes. Wednesday. At the Cantina over on Ashland and Roosevelt?"

"The one with the fresh tortillas and the great margaritas?" She smiled.

He broke out into a silly grin. "Yes, that one. Sounds like a plan. How about noon?"

"Make it twelve thirty, and it's a deal."

As she walked away, she felt like a little bit of heaven had just opened up.

Michael was surprised at how nervous and edgy he was. On the way to the restaurant, he started to pick up some flowers. He actually told the taxi to stop by the florist and got out to go into the store before changing his mind and getting back in the taxi. He didn't want to overdo it, and he certainly didn't want anything to remind him or her of their last encounter at the hospital.

After he left her that day six months ago, something happened to him. He'd plunged into his work with more vigor than ever. He almost single-handedly brought down the governor in the truck licensing scandal. And he stopped using women as he had been. He dated a couple of times, but that was all. His new life was a routine of work, gym, and time with his family. But something was still missing. There was what felt like a hole in his heart. An empty place that needed filling was the only way he could describe it to himself. He was just sure that whatever it was he needed, he wouldn't find it in meaningless relationships and booze.

He arrived at the Cantina at twelve fifteen. He didn't know why he felt so strongly about seeing Kenisha again. He thought that he must be hanging onto guilt, and if she forgave him, he would be released from it. He was waiting for her in the foyer. The restaurant was crowded, but they moved the crowd in and out quickly and efficiently. There was still plenty of seating when Kenisha came in, beautiful to his eyes in a black wool coat with a softly draped hood. It was her smile, though, that he saw.

"Hi, Michael, it's good to see you. I really am happy you could have lunch with me. Have you been waiting long?" Her smile seemed to beam happiness like a laser, cutting right through the layers of guilt, worry, and nervousness, bringing healing and joy into his heart.

Michael had been holding his breath without realizing it and was finally able to breathe. He smiled back. "Kenisha. It's good to see you, too. No, I just got here a few minutes ago."

The waiter ushered them to a two-person table, gave them menus, and put a bowl of freshly made tortilla chips and salsa in front of them.

Kenisha was the first to speak. "Michael, I want to apologize to you. I should have been more understanding when you came to visit me in the hospital. I was just in a lot of pain right then. And not only the physical pain. I blamed myself for what happened to Joe, and I felt like I needed somebody else to blame, too."

He started to interrupt her. "You don't have to apolo—"

She broke in. "Please let me finish, Michael. I do need to apologize for so many things. I should have listened to you in the hospital. I should have thanked you then for trying to save Joe and for helping with Kisha. I should have called you to thank you when I realized that Joe's business wouldn't be brought up in that hired truck trial. When I finally worked through my grief and realized that none of us is at fault for what happened to Joe, I should have called you and apologized then. I don't know why I didn't do that. But when I saw you Monday, I knew that now was the right time for me to offer an apology for all that I've done wrong to you. Will you please accept it?" She looked at him with something in her eyes that he had not seen before. What he saw was more than her usual caring and joy; it was something profound and deep that he couldn't quite name.

His eyes shone with sincerity. "You don't have to apologize, Kenisha. I'm the one who needs to apologize. I should have at least warned you of what might happen if Joe decided to wear the wire. I was trying to protect you and your family, and I made a mess of it. I should have gotten there faster. Maybe I should have called the police ahead of me. I couldn't fix the problem I created in your life, and I'm so sorry."

When the waiter came over to the table, they realized that they had not even looked at the menus. They told him just a few minutes.

She said, "That's enough, Michael." She smiled and waved a

napkin in his direction. "I accept your apology, and I absolve you of all wrongdoing. Will you do the same for me?"

"Thank you for forgiving me." He smiled and then waved his napkin over her head. "And I hereby absolve you of all wrongdoing toward me."

As they laughed together, her napkin fell to the floor. They reached down at the same time to pick it up and, aiming to grab the napkin, he grabbed her hand. Something happened when their hands touched. In that split second, the touch revealed to them a truth that they both felt. In that moment under the table they both recognized something so real that it could be neither explained nor denied. They looked into each other's eyes and lingered there. They would later describe it as love at first touch. But then there were no words, just an understanding that they both knew when they looked in each other's eyes. When they brought themselves up from under the table, they stopped smiling and seemed almost embarrassed as they continued to look at each other, searching for words and finding none adequate.

The waiter's return to fill their water glasses broke the spell, and their response to his request for their order was to laugh, again. Their souls within sang healthy and healing joy. They remembered as much as they would be able to remember in the created world. They didn't remember that they were Angels. They remembered that they were meant to be together.

The End.

LaVergne, TN USA
30 September 2010
199116LV00001B/7/P

9 781450 251457